"十三五"国家重点出版规划项目

李白诗歌全集英译

A Complete Edition of Pai Li's Poems in Chinese and English
With Annotations

赵彦春 译·注
Translated and Annotated by Yanchun Chao

第四卷
Volume IV

上海大学出版社
·上海·

卷 四

目 录
Contents

729　**古近体诗三十二首**
　　Old-new Rhythmic Poetry, 32 Poems

731　赠王判官，时余归隐，居庐山屏风叠
　　To Wang, a Military Judge from Overlapped Screens of Mt. Lodge, Where I Live in Reclusion

734　在水军宴赠幕府诸侍御
　　To the Military Judges at the Navy Feast

737　赠武十七谔并序
　　To O Wu Seventeen with a Preface

739　赠闾丘宿松
　　To Ch'iu Lü, Magistrate of Lodge Pine

741　狱中上崔相涣
　　To Premier Huan Ts'ui When I'm in Prison

743　中丞宋公以吴兵三千赴河南军次寻阳脱余之囚
　　Mid-supervisor Sung Set Me Free from the Jail When He Led Three Thousand Wu Soldiers to Honan and Then to Bankshine

745　流夜郎赠辛判官
　　Presented to Judge Hsin When I Was Exiled to Nightboy

747　赠刘都使
　　To Adviser Liu

749　赠常侍御
　　To Ch'ang, the Royal Servant

751　赠易秀才
　　To Ee, the Showcharm

753	经乱离后天恩流夜郎忆旧游书怀赠江夏韦太守良宰	
	To Liangtsai Wei, Prefect of Riversummer, My Old Friend, When I Am Exiled to Nightboy at the Time of Unrest	
766	江夏使君叔席上赠史郎中	
	To Vice Minister Shih at a Feast Hosted by My Uncle, Prefect of Riversummer	
768	博平郑太守自庐山千里相寻入江夏北市门见访，却之武陵，立马赠别	
	An Impromptu to Prefect Cheng of Broadpeace Coming All the Way to Riversummer from Mt. Lodge and Seeing Me Off to Martial Ridge at North Market Gate	
771	江上赠窦长史	
	To T'ou, Chief of Staff When I'm on the River	
773	赠王汉阳	
	To Wang, Magistrate of Hanshine	
775	赠汉阳辅录事二首	
	To Secretary Fu of Hanshine, Two Poems	
778	江夏赠韦南陵冰	
	To Ice Wei, a Magistrate of Southridge, from Riversummer	
782	赠卢司户	
	To Lu, a Household Registrar	
783	赠从弟南平太守之遥二首	
	To Chihyao Li, My Cousin, Magistrate of Southpeace, Two Poems	
787	赠潘侍御论钱少阳	
	To P'an, the Royal Censor, an Evaluation of Firstshine Ch'ien	
789	赠柳圆	
	To Yüan Liu	
791	流夜郎半道承恩放还兼欣克复之美书怀示息秀才	
	To Hsi, a Showcharm, When I'm Set Free on My Way to Nightboy and Hear of the Restoration	
795	赠张相镐	
	To Premier Hao Chang	
804	闻谢杨儿吟猛虎词，因此有赠	
	Hearing Yang'er Hsieh Singing *A Tiger*, Hence the Poem	

805	宿清溪主人
	In Blue Stream I Stay
806	系寻阳上崔相涣三首
	To Premier Ts'ui in Bankshine, Three Poems
809	巴陵赠贾舍人
	To Secretary Chia at Paridge

811	**古近体诗二十五首**
	Old-new Rhythmic Poetry, 25 Poems
813	赠别舍人弟台卿之江南
	Seeing Off Brother, Secretary T'aich'ing to South
816	醉后赠王历阳
	To Wang, Magistrate of Leeshine after I'm Drunk
818	赠历阳褚司马，时此公为稚子舞，故作是诗也
	To Ssuma Ch'u in Leeshine, Who Dances a Child's Dance, Hence My Poem
820	对雪醉后赠王历阳
	To Magistrate Wang of Leeshine When I'm Drunk in Snow
822	赠宣城宇文太守兼呈崔侍御
	To Yüwen, Magistrate of Hsuan While Presented to Royal Servant Ts'ui
830	赠宣城赵太守悦
	To Yüeh Chao, Magistrate of Hsuan
835	赠从弟宣州长史昭
	To My Cousin, Glare, Secretary of Hsuan
838	于五松山赠南陵常赞府
	To Ch'ang, Magistrate of Southridge, at Mt. Five Pines
841	自梁园至敬亭山见会公谈陵阳山水兼期同游因有此赠
	Coming to See Mr. Hui at Mt. Ching't'ing, Talking About Hills and Rills of Ridgeshine and Hoping to Tour There Together, Hence the Poem
845	赠友人三首
	To My Friends, Three Poems
852	陈情赠友人
	To My Friend, A Plaint

| 856 | 赠从弟洌 |
| | To Li Li, My Cousin |

| 859 | 赠间丘处士 |
| | To Staff Knoll Lü |

| 861 | 赠钱征君少阳 |
| | To Firstshine Ch'ien, a Recruit Not Accepting the Post |

| 863 | 赠宣州灵源寺仲浚公 |
| | To Master Chün Chung at Soul Source Temple in Hsuan |

| 865 | 赠僧朝美 |
| | To Mei Ch'ao, the Monk |

| 867 | 赠僧行融 |
| | To Jung Hsing, the Monk |

| 869 | 赠黄山胡公求白鹇 |
| | To Mr. Hu at Mt. Yellow, Who Gives Me Silver Pheasants as a Gift |

| 871 | 登敬亭山南望怀古赠窦主簿 |
| | To Secretary T'ou When, Having Climbed Up Mt. Chingt'ing, I Gaze South While Thinking of the Past |

| 874 | 经乱后将避地剡中留赠崔宣城 |
| | To Ts'ui, Magistrate of Hsuan When I Seek Shelter in Mid-Shan at the Time of Unrest |

| 878 | 献从叔当涂宰阳冰 |
| | To Sun Ice Li, My Uncle, Magistrate of Tangt'u |

| 884 | 书怀赠南陵常赞府 |
| | To Ts'ang, Magistrate of Southridge |

| 888 | 赠汪伦 |
| | To Lun Wang |

| 889 | **古近体诗二十五首** |
| | Old-new Rhythmic Poetry, 25 Poems |

| 891 | 安陆白兆山桃花岩寄刘侍御绾 |
| | Sent to Wan Liu, the Royal Servant from the Peach Blossom Mound, the Paichao Hills, Anlu |

894	淮南卧病书怀寄蜀中赵征君蕤	
	Sent to Jui Chao, a Recruit When I Am Ill in Huainan	
897	寄弄月溪吴山人	
	To Wu, a Hermit at the Moonplay Stream	
899	秋山寄卫尉张卿及王征君	
	Sent from a Hill in Autumn to Guard Commander Chang and Wang, a Recruit	
901	望终南山寄紫阁隐者	
	Sent to the Hermit in Purple Chamber in the Southern Hills	
903	夕霁杜陵登楼寄韦繇	
	To Yao Wei, Climbing up a Tower on Birchleaf Pear Ridge After a Sunlit Rain	
905	秋夜宿龙门香山寺,奉寄王方城十七丈,奉国莹上人,从弟幼成、令问	
	To Senior Wang Seventeen, Magistrate of Squareton, and Ying Kuo, a Monk, Also to My Cousins, Youch'eng and Lingwen When I Am in Balm Hill Temple at Dragongate for an Autumn Night	
908	春日独坐寄郑明府	
	Sent to Magistrate Cheng on a Lonely Spring Day	
910	寄淮南友人	
	Sent to My Friend in Huainan	
912	沙丘城下寄杜甫	
	To Fu Tu from a Town Called Sandknoll	
914	闻丹丘子于城北营石门幽居,中有高凤遗迹,仆离群远怀,亦有栖遁之志,因叙旧以寄之	
	A Recall Dedicated to Redknoll, Who Lived at Stonegate North of the Town, Where One Could See Hiphoenix's Trace. I, a Vagrant, Would Also Retire	
918	淮阴书怀寄王宋城	
	Sent to Wang, Magistrate of Sungton from Huaishade	
921	闻王昌龄左迁龙标遥有此寄	
	To Ch'angling Wang upon His Demotion	
922	寄王屋山人孟大融	
	Sent to Tajung Meng, an Immortal on Mt. King's Hood	

924		忆旧游寄谯郡元参军
		Sent To Staff Yüan in Chiao County, a Recall of My Friend
930		月夜江行寄崔员外宗之
		Sent to Tsungchih Ts'ui, a Standby, When I'm on a Moonlit River Tour
932		宿白鹭洲寄杨江宁
		To Magistrate Yang When I Put Up for the Night on Egret Shoal
934		新林浦阳风寄友人
		To My Friend from Newshore in the Wind
936		寄韦南陵冰,余江上乘兴访之,遇寻颜尚书笑有此赠
		To Ice Wei, Magistrate of Southridge, Whom I Meet and Greet While Rowing Upstream and with a Laugh Give This Poem
939		题情深树寄象公
		To Mr. Hsiang, Dedication to a Loving Tree
940		北山独酌寄韦六
		Sent to Wei Six While I Drink Alone at North Hill
942		寄当涂赵少府炎
		Sent to Yan Chao, a County Sheriff of Tangt'u
943		寄东鲁二稚子
		Sent to My Two Children in the East of Lu
946		独酌清溪江石上寄权昭夷
		Sent to Chao-ee Ch'üan While I Drink on Mother Boulder in the Clear Stream
948		禅房怀友人岑伦
		To Lun Tsen, My Friend
951		**古近体诗二十六首**
		Old-new Rhythmic Poetry, 26 Poems
953		庐山谣寄卢侍御虚舟
		A Mt. Lodge Ballad to Void Boat Lu, a Royal Servant
956		下寻阳城泛彭蠡寄黄判官
		Sent to Huang the Judge When I Am at Lake Gourd, Bankshine

958	书情寄从弟邠州长史昭 Sent to My Cousin, Glare, Staff of Fenchow
960	寄王汉阳 Sent to Wang, Magistrate of Hanshine
961	春日归山寄孟浩然 Sent to Haojan Meng When I Return to the Hills on a Spring Day
963	流夜郎永华寺寄寻阳群官 Sent to the Officials in Bankshine from E'er Flora Fane in Nightboy
965	流夜郎至西塞驿寄裴隐 Sent to Yin P'ei When I Arrive at the Border West on My Way to Nightboy
967	自汉阳病酒归寄王明府 Sent to Magistrate Wang When I'm Back from Hanshine, Ill and Drunk
969	望汉阳柳色寄王宰 Sent to Magistrate Wang When I View Willows by the Hanshine River
970	江夏寄汉阳辅录事 Sent to Fu, an Office Clerk, in Hanshine, Riversummer
973	早春寄王汉阳 Sent to Wang, Magistrate of Hanshine in Early Spring
975	江上寄巴东故人 Sent to My Friend in East Pa from the River
977	江上寄元六林宗 Sent to Lintzung Yüan Six from the River
979	寄从弟宣州长史昭 Sent to Glare Li, My Cousin, Secretary General of Hsuan
980	泾溪东亭寄郑少府谔 Sent to O Cheng, Sheriff from East Pavilion at the Ching Stream
982	宣州九日闻崔四侍御与宇文太守游敬亭，余时登响山，不同此赏，醉后寄崔侍御 Two Poems Sent To Ts'ui, the Royal Servant, When I'm Drunk. I've Been in Hsuan for Nine Days, Where I Hear Ts'ui Climb Mt. Ching t'ing with Prefect Yüwen While I Climb Mt. Loud

987 寄崔侍御
    To Ts'ui, the Royal Servant

989 泾溪南蓝山下有落星潭,可以卜筑,余泊舟石上,寄何判官昌浩
    Sent to Boom Ho, a Judge. There's Star Gulping Abyss Below Mt. Blue South of the Ching Stream, Where One Can Divine. I Moor My Boat at a Boulder

991 早过漆林渡寄万巨
    Sent to Chü Wan at Lacquer Ford Early in the Morning

993 游敬亭寄崔侍御
    Sent to Ts'ui, the Royal Servant, While I'm in Mt. Chingt'ing

995 三山望金陵寄殷淑
    Sent to Shu Yin, Looking at Gold Hill from Mt. Three

996 自金陵溯流过白璧山玩月达天门寄句容王主簿
    Sent to Wang, Secretary of Chüjung, When I Go Upstream from Gold Hill, Pass Mt. White Disc and Arrive at Heaven Gate to View the Moon

998 寄上吴王三首
    To King of Wu, Three Poems

古近体诗三十二首
Old-new Rhythmic Poetry, 32 Poems

赠王判官，时余归隐，居庐山屏风叠

昔别黄鹤楼，
蹉跎淮海秋。
俱飘零落叶，
各散洞庭流。
中年不相见，
蹭蹬游吴越。
何处我思君？
天台绿萝月。
会稽风月好，
却绕剡溪回。
云山海上出，
人物镜中来。
一度浙江北，
十年醉楚台。
荆门倒屈宋，
梁苑倾邹枚。
苦笑我夸诞，
知音安在哉？
大盗割鸿沟，
如风扫秋叶。
吾非济代人，
且隐屏风叠。
中夜天中望，
忆君思见君。
明朝拂衣去，
永与海鸥群。

To Wang, a Military Judge from Overlapped Screens of Mt. Lodge, Where I Live in Reclusion

From Yellow Crane Tower we did part;
Thru Huaihai's autumn loafs my heart.
Then like fallen leaves we were blown;
Now with Cavehall's waves we have flown.
Mid-aged, we can't together be;
This southern land does worry me.
Where do you think I for you croon?
In Mt. Heaven lit by the moon.
Mt. Summit's so good, like a dream,
So surrounded by the Shan Stream.
From the sea clouded hills come here;
In the glass some figures appear.
Since I left the Ch'ient'ang's waves then,
I've drunk on Ch'u Mound for years ten.
My flair does Ch'ü and Sung o'erpower;
Tsou and Mei before my art cower.
No one can match me, so I jeer;
Where is my companion, o where?
The land's been torn by heinous thieves,
Like an autumn wind sweeping leaves.
To save the state I'm not the one;
Behind the screens the fires I shun.
I look at the sky at midnight,
Thinking of you in my dire plight.
At dawn I'll from here go away;

With seagulls for ever I'll stay.

* Overlapped Screens: a picturesque peak of Mt. Lodge, which looks like screens overlapped.
* Mt. Lodge: a famous mountain with historic, cultural and religious attractions, located in present-day Chianghsi Province, though not belonging to the Five Mountains consecrated in Chinese history.
* Yellow Crane Tower: a famous tower built in the Three Kingdom period, in present-day Wuhan, Hupei Province.
* Huaihai: indicating an area covering present-day Chiangsu, Shantung, Anhui and Honan provinces.
* Cavehall: referring to Lake Cavehall, a lake in Hunan Province.
* Mt. Heaven: the birthplace of Heaven sect of Chinese Buddhism and southern sect of Wordism, located in present-day Chechiang Province.
* Mt. Summit: the K'uaichi Mountains in present-day Chechiang Province, where Worm convened a summit attended by vassal lords, hence the name.
* the Shan Stream: a main stream with rich cultural attractions in present-day Shengchow, Chechiang Province.
* Ch'ient'ang: the lower part of the Zigzag River, the largest river in today's Chechiang Province.
* Ch'ü: referring to Yüan Ch'ü (340 B.C.- 278 B.C.), a great patriotic poet and official of Ch'u, who threw himself into the Milo River, so aggrieved at his broken state.
* Sung: referring to Jade Sung, a student of Yüan Ch'ü. In the myths, King Huai of Ch'u once met Goddess of Mt. Witch and had an intercourse overnight in his dream. Jade Sung recorded the story in *Verse to T'ang* when he traveled with King Hsiang to Mt. Witch.
* Tsou: referring to Tsou Yang, a litterateur with high reputation in the Western Han dynasty.
* Mei: referring to Cheng Mei (? - 140 B.C.), a renowned verse writer in the Western Han dynasty.
* seagull: a kind of sea bird, any gull or large tern, a symbol of clean integrity. The seagulls in the Wordist book *Sir Line* (Liehtzu) are particularly sensitive to impurity of motive and will make friends only with the completely guileless and disinterested.

在水军宴赠幕府诸侍御

月化五白龙，
翻飞凌九天。
胡沙惊北海，
电扫洛阳川。
虏箭雨宫阙，
皇舆成播迁。
英王受庙略，
秉钺清南边。
云旗卷海雪，
金戟罗江烟。
聚散百万人，
弛张在一贤。
霜台降群彦，
水国奉戎旃。
绣服开宴语，
天人借楼船。
如登黄金台，
遥谒紫霞仙。
卷身编蓬下，
冥机四十年。
宁知草间人，
腰下有龙泉？
浮云在一决，
誓欲清幽燕。
愿与四座公，
静谈金匮篇。
齐心戴朝恩，

不惜微躯捐。
所冀虏头灭,
功成追鲁连。

To the Military Judges at the Navy Feast

The white dragon the moon does eye,
And to the Ninth Sky it will fly.
The Hun sandstorm does North Sea scare,
Like lightning sweeps o'er the Lo there.
The arrows hit the towers like rain;
Lord and peers flee, lo cart and wain.
The wise prince at the court's order
Pacifies the southern border.
The flags whoosh up the ocean snow;
The spears see the Lo River flow.
A million troops he does command,
To run so fast or firmly stand.
Many talents come to Frost Mound;
Vast water hears flags' flapping sound.
The silken gowns the feast attend;
The prince to them his warships lend.
As if a golden mound they climb
To overlook clouds o'er the clime.
In the thatched cottage there I hide,
For forty years, all laid aside.
Who knows someone there lying waste,
A Dragon Spring sword on his waist?
All the floating clouds he will sweep
And across Dim Yan he will leap.

For peers to sit around I'd look
So we could discuss *Golden Book*.
With one heart we'll repay His grace,
Marching to battlefields apace.
To quell the revolt we decide
And then in the hills we'll abide.

* The moon the white dragon does eye: implying Lushan An's ambition when he revolted. According to the explanations of ancient oneiromancy, the moon implies an official and the white dragon represents the king or emperor. If the moon covets the dragon, it means that there will be an official trying to usurp the throne.
* the Ninth Sky: the high sky, the vast empyrean, the highest of the nine layers of the sky according to Chinese legend.
* Hun: one of barbaric nomadic Asian peoples who frequently invaded China, a general term referring to all northern or western invaders or aliens.
* the wise prince: indicating Prince E'er (? - A.D. 757), the 16th son of Emperor Deepsire of T'ang. He was assigned to guard the south during Lushan An's Rebellion.
* Frost Mound: an alternative name for censorate.
* Dragon Spring sword: a legendary sword made by Yehtzu Ou, a renowned swordsmith.
* Dim Yan: referring to the base area of Lushan An's army, covering present-day Peking, Tientsin, northern part of Hopei and western part of Liaoning and some area of North Korea, which is north of the Daedong River.
* *Golden Book*: a book about the art of war, a book in two volumes written by Tzuya Chiang (also known as Great Grand), an influential strategist and statesman.

赠武十七谔并序

门人武谔,深于义者也。质本沉悍,慕要离之风,潜钓川海,不数数于世间事,闻中原作难,西来访余。余爱子伯禽在鲁,许将冒胡兵以致之,酒酣感激援笔而赠。

马如一匹练,
明日过吴门。
乃是要离客,
西来欲报恩。
笑开燕匕首,
拂拭竟无言。
狄犬吠清洛,
天津成塞垣。
爱子隔东鲁,
空悲断肠猿。
林回弃白璧,
千里阻同奔。
君为我致之,
轻赍涉淮原。
精诚合天道,
不愧远游魂。

To O Wu Seventeen with a Preface

My disciple called O Wu is a righteous man. He, steady and fierce, admires Yaolee, an assassin. He goes fishing, unconcerned with world affairs. When he heard of the upheaval, he came west to pay me a visit. As my son Firstling Bird was stranded in Shantung, he ran the risk of being captured by the Huns to save him. I am gratified now drunk, hence the poem.

> His horse that glimmers like cloth white
> At dawn will pass Wu Gate in flight.
> He, an assassin like Yaolee,
> Comes west to pay respect to me.
> He shows his dagger with a smile
> And falls silent for quite a while.
> The Hun dogs run wild in the town;
> Kingford Bridge is there, fallen down.
> My son's stranded in Shantung there;
> I scream like an ape in despair.
> He throws away jade and his pack
> And runs here, my son on his back.
> You have done that just for my sake,
> Thru all dangers from plain to lake.
> Your worth befits the Word divine,
> A ghost you are, a ghost so fine.

* Yaolee: an assassin of Wu who refused to be awarded after his successful assassination.
* Shantung: Shantung in T'ang times meant the area south of the Yellow River, covering today's Shantung, Chiangsu, northern Anhui and some part of Honan.
* the Hun dogs: referring to Lushan An's soldiers.
* Kingford Bridge: a bridge of great importance in Loshine, which connected two prosperous blocks of the ancient city.
* the Word: referring to Tao if transliterated, the most significant and profoundest concept in Chinese philosophy. According to Laocius's *The Word and the World*: "The Word is void, but its use is infinite. O deep! It seems to be the root of all things." The Word is identifiable with the Word or Logos in the West, as there is an enormous amount of common ground in the two cosmologies and the doctrines concerning the most fundamental matters such as "the Word is the One" and "God is the One", and the personalization of Being, the progenitor of finite spirits, which are subordinate kinds of Being or merely appearances of the Divine, the One.

赠闾丘宿松

阮籍为太守，
乘驴上东平。
剖竹十日间，
一朝风化清。
偶来拂衣去，
谁测主人情。
夫子理宿松，
浮云知古城。
扫地物莽然，
秋来百草生。
飞鸟还旧巢，
迁人返躬耕。
何惭宓子贱，
不减陶渊明。
吾知千载后，
却掩二贤名。

To Ch'iu Lü, Magistrate of Lodge Pine

In East Peace Chi Juan would preside,
A prefect, of an ass astride.
Within ten days, he tore the room wall
And cleansed the office above all.
He left, his sleeves flowing beside;
Who can guess what thoughts he did hide?
Now you're magistrate of Lodge Pine;

E'en clouds know this town is so fine.
The ground is so lush everywhere;
In autumn grass grows here and there.
The stray birds fly back to their nest;
The refugees farm again with zest.
With Tzuch'ien Mi you can compare,
And can match T'ao, alias Glare.
Then, in a thousand years, your name,
I am sure, will eclipse their fame.

* Lodge Pine: a county located in the southwest of today's Anhui Province.
* East Peace: a county located in the southwest of today's Shantung Province.
* Chi Juan: Chi Juan (A.D. 210 – A.D. 263), a poet of the Three Kingdoms period and one of the Seven Sages of the Bamboo Grove.
* ass: any of a number of horselike perissodactylous mammals (family *Equidae*) having long ears used as a metaphor for a person as obstinate and stupid.
* Tzuch'ien Mi: Tzuch'ien Mi (521 B.C.– 445 B.C.), a prized student of Confucius. As its magistrate, he governed Shan County well.
* T'ao: referring to Ch'ien T'ao (A.D. 352 – A.D. 427) or Yüanming Tao if transliterated, a verse writer, poet, and litterateur in the Chin dynasty, and the founder of Chinese idyllism. He was once the magistrate of P'engtse, but he resigned four times to live in reclusion. All in all, he can be remembered as a complex figure and a poet of complex poems, as has been termed by J. P. Seaton.

狱中上崔相涣

胡马渡洛水，
血流征战场。
千门闭秋景，
万姓危朝霜。
贤相燮元气，
再欣海县康。
台庭有夔龙，
列宿粲成行。
羽翼三元圣，
发辉两太阳。
应念覆盆下，
雪泣拜天光。

To Premier Huan Ts'ui When I'm in Prison

The Hun horses did the Lo wade;
The Huns our soldiers fiercely slayed.
To the autumn all doors were closed;
The folks felt cold in dawning frost.
Now, premier, with might you arrive
And will again make the land thrive.
The court boasts you, a mastermind,
With sparkling stars afore aligned.
The three saints you shield with respect;
With care the two suns you protect.

> But in the dungeon I've no light,
> Now waiting for your sunshine bright.

* the Hun horses: a metonymy for Lushan An's troops. Lushan An, a powerful general-governor of T'ang, was of foreign extraction, descended from a family of Iranian warriors, his mother being a Turkish witch.
* the two suns: referring to the two emperors in the upheaval of Lushan An's Rebellion. Emperor Deepsire of T'ang abdicated in favor of the crown prince, his third son.
* dungeon: a dark underground cell, vault or prison, sometimes used as a metaphor for the hell or Hades.

中丞宋公以吴兵三千赴河南军次寻阳脱余之囚

独坐清天下，
专征出海隅。
九江皆渡虎，
三郡尽还珠。
组练明秋浦，
楼船入郢都。
风高初选将，
月满欲平胡。
杀气横千里，
军声动九区。
白猿惭剑术，
黄石借兵符。
戎虏行当翦，
鲸鲵立可诛。
自怜非剧孟，
何以佐良图。

Mid-supervisor Sung Set Me Free from the Jail When He Led Three Thousand Wu Soldiers to Honan and Then to Bankshine

In your office you judge with care;
Now you lead troops to the coast there.
The Nine Rivers' waves can't you cow;
The three counties all to you bow.

To Autumn Shore your soldiers glow;
Out of Ying Town your warships row.
In high wind you select best ones;
In moonlight you defeat the Huns.
Your killing shouts the vast land quake;
Your marching roars the nine realms shake.
White Ape to your swordsmanship bends;
Yellow Stone his book to you lends.
The Huns will before you perish;
The whales you will shortly finish.
Pity, I don't have Chümeng's might;
How can I help to set things right?

* The Nine Rivers: Bankshine, that is today's Chiuchiang, Chianghsi Province.
* Autumn Shore: a county in today's Anhui Province, a place rich in silver and copper resources.
* White Ape: As is said, in the State of Yüeh, there was a girl good at swordplay. She once met an old man who called himself White Ape and asked for a competition in swordplay. As they finished the fight, the old man turned into an ape and went away.
* Yellow Stone: a legendary Wordist at the foot of Mt. Hub Town, who gave Liang Chang *The Art of War*, which played a decisive part in the latter's life and in the founding of the Han dynasty.
* Chümeng: a gallant in the Fore-Ch'in period, who often saved people from danger.
* whale: a cetaceous mammal of fish-like form, especially one of the giant pelagic species, as distinguished from dolphins and porpoises. Whales have the fore limbs developed as broad flattened paddles, hind limbs absent, and a thick layer of fat or blubber immediately beneath the skin. A whale is a symbol of great ambition, fortitude and uniqueness.

流夜郎赠辛判官

昔在长安醉花柳,
五侯七贵同杯酒。
气岸遥凌豪士前,
风流肯落他人后?
夫子红颜我少年,
章台走马著金鞭。
文章献纳麒麟殿,
歌舞淹留玳瑁筵。
与君自谓长如此,
宁知草动风尘起。
函谷忽惊胡马来,
秦宫桃李向明开。
我愁远谪夜郎去,
何日金鸡放赦回?

Presented to Judge Hsin When I Was Exiled to Nightboy

Before, with buds and blooms I'd drink and dine;
Lords and peers shared with me a cup of wine.
My pride overrode those proud and refined;
In rosy life how could I fall behind?
A young man, I would oft show off my flair
While galloping fast thru the thoroughfare.
To the Lord I'd offer my verse of romance,
And was treated with a feast, song or dance.

I thought my life could carry on like this
While grass was blown up with something amiss.
Alarming, the Huns poured in from Case Dale;
Plums and peaches at court tried to prevail.
Sad, I was exiled to Nightboy there, alack;
When, with an amnesty, could I go back?

* Case Dale: an ancient pass located to the east of the capital, and Lint'ao to the west, once the border of the State of Ch'in.
* Nightboy: once the biggest kingdom founded by southern barbarians in the southwest existing from the Warring States period to the Han dynasty, which was a provincial malarial land to Han Chinese. When a Han envoy visited Nigthboy, the king asked: "Which is bigger, Nigthboy or Han?" This self-important question has been a laughing stock ever since. In 27 B.C., Nightboy was wiped out by Han and was made a county.

赠刘都使

东平刘公幹，
南国秀馀芳。
一鸣即朱绂，
五十佩银章。
饮冰事戎幕，
衣锦华水乡。
铜官几万人，
诤讼清玉堂。
吐言贵珠玉，
落笔回风霜。
而我谢明主，
衔哀投夜郎。
归家酒债多，
门客粲成行。
高谈满四座，
一日倾千觞。
所求竟无绪，
裘马欲摧藏。
主人若不顾，
明发钓沧浪。

To Adviser Liu

You are a Liu of East Peace, grand,
A balmy flower in Southern Land.
How great, you set the world on fire;

At fifty you're promoted higher.
In the north you worked as an aide
And now have come back in brocade.
Tens of thousands of people there,
You settle all, so square and fair.
You speak with words like shining pearls,
And write so fast, like a wind whirls.
I thank the Lord who was so mild;
To Nightboy there I was exiled.
I came back home in debt of wine;
My hangers-on formed a long line.
My guests all talked in a big way;
A thousand cups were drunk a day.
Soon, I was running out of gold;
Furs and horses I could not hold.
Sir, if you don't lend me a hand,
Tomorrow I will roam the land.

* pearl: a smooth, lustrous, usually white and bluish-gray, calcareous concretion deposited in layers around a central nucleus in the shells of various mollusks or oysters, and largely used as a gem, medicine or given as a gift, a metaphor for the dearest one, a representation of nobility, purity and dignity in Chinese culture.
* Nightboy: Yelang if transliterated, once the biggest country in the southwest existing till the Han dynasty, covering today's Kuichow, West Hunan and North Kuanghsi. In 27 B.C., Nightboy, which was a provincial malarial land to Han Chinese, was wiped out by the Han Empire and was instituted as a county.
* Liu of East Peace: referring to Chen Liu (A.D. 180 – A.D. 217), one of the Seven Scholars in the age of Making Peace (A.D. 196 – A.D. 220), who was born in East Peace (a county located in the southwest of today's Shantung Province).

赠常侍御

安石在东山，
无心济天下。
一起振横流，
功成复潇洒。
大贤有卷舒，
季叶轻风雅。
匡复属何人，
君为知音者。
传闻武安将，
气振长平瓦。
燕赵期洗清，
周秦保宗社。
登朝若有言，
为访南迁贾。

To Ch'ang, the Royal Servant

Steady Stone was at the East Hill;
To serve the world he had no will.
With one blow, all he pacified;
Successful, he'd play, glorified.
A great sage may go free, rest or rise;
The world does elegance despise.
To win, on whom can we depend?
On you, for you are my best friend.
I hear when War Peace snored awake,

　　　　　The tiles over his head would break.
　　　　　The northern states need to be swept;
　　　　　So that fanes and shrines can be kept.
　　　　　Whene'er you go to court, my friend,
　　　　　This exiled one please recommend.

* Steady Stone: referring to An Hsieh (A.D. 320 – A.D. 385), so called because he was the living stone of the country. He was a general, a statesman and renowned scholar in the Eastern Chin dynasty.
* The East Hill: the East Hills, located in Shaohsing, a place for reclusion, where An Hsieh (A.D. 320 – A.D. 385) used to live.
* War Peace: the title conferred to White Rise (Pai Ch'i), one of the Four Commanders in the Warring States period, strategist of the State of Ch'in.

赠易秀才

少年解长剑，
投赠即分离。
何不断犀象？
精光暗往时。
蹉跎君自惜，
窜逐我因谁？
地远虞翻老，
秋深宋玉悲。
空摧芳桂色，
不屈古松姿。
感激平生意，
劳歌寄此辞。

To Ee, the Showcharm

You, a young man, a sword you play;
As a gift, you give it away.
Shall I cut tusk or rhino horn?
Unlike before, I'm weak and worn.
Time flies, of yourself do take care;
For whom am I exiled, whoe'er?
Fan Yü was banished far away;
Jade Sung cried to the autumn day.
When laurels fade, on the decline,
I still stand upright like a pine.
Thank you very much for your love;

I'll sing a song for all above.

* showcharm: a talent recommended for official use through civil service examinations, or a well learned person in ancient China. Showcharms are primary candidates, who have passed civil service examinations at provincial level, followed by more advanced recommendees (chüjen), offerees (kungshi), and enterees (chinshi). Showcharm are very well respected in a meritocratic and bureaucratic society like China.
* Fan Yü (A.D. 164 – A.D. 233): a scholar and official in the Three Kingdoms period. He was once exiled for giving bold advice to King of Wu.
* Jade Sung: Jade Sung (cir. 298 B.C.– cir. 222 B.C.), a student of Yüan Ch'ü's, and a verse writer in the Warring States period. He once served as an official for King Hsiang of Ch'u. When King Hsiang traveled to Clouds Moor, he promised his retinues a farmland in Clouds Moor if any of them could write a verse, and Sung with his brilliant verse won the land.

经乱离后天恩流夜郎忆旧游书怀赠江夏韦太守良宰

天上白玉京，
十二楼五城。
仙人抚我顶，
结发受长生。
误逐世间乐，
颇穷理乱情。
九十六圣君，
浮云挂空名。
天地赌一掷，
未能忘战争。
试涉霸王略，
将期轩冕荣。
时命乃大谬，
弃之海上行。
学剑翻自哂，
为文竟何成。
剑非万人敌，
文窃四海声。
儿戏不足道，
五噫出西京。
临当欲去时，
慷慨泪沾缨。
叹君倜傥才，
标举冠群英。
开筵引祖帐，
慰此远徂征。

鞍马若浮云，
送余骠骑亭。
歌钟不尽意，
白日落昆明。
十月到幽州，
戈鋋若罗星。
君王弃北海，
扫地借长鲸。
呼吸走百川，
燕然可摧倾。
心知不得语，
却欲栖蓬瀛。
弯弧惧天狼，
挟矢不敢张。
揽涕黄金台，
呼天哭昭王。
无人贵骏骨，
绿耳空腾骧。
乐毅倘再生，
于今亦奔亡。
蹉跎不得意，
驱马过贵乡。
逢君听弦歌，
肃穆坐华堂。
百里独太古，
陶然卧羲皇。
征乐昌乐馆，
开筵列壶觞。
贤豪间青娥，
对烛俨成行。
醉舞纷绮席，

清歌绕飞梁。
欢娱未终朝,
秩满归咸阳。
祖道拥万人,
供帐遥相望。
一别隔千里,
荣枯异炎凉。
炎凉几度改,
九土中横溃。
汉甲连胡兵,
沙尘暗云海。
草木摇杀气,
星辰无光彩。
白骨成丘山,
苍生竟何罪。
函关壮帝居,
国命悬哥舒。
长戟三十万,
开门纳凶渠。
公卿如犬羊,
忠谠醢与菹。
二圣出游豫,
两京遂丘墟。
帝子许专征,
秉旄控强楚。
节制非桓文,
军师拥熊虎。
人心失去就,
贼势腾风雨。
惟君固房陵,
诚节冠终古。

仆卧香炉顶,
餐霞漱瑶泉。
门开九江转,
枕下五湖连。
半夜水军来,
浔阳满旌旃。
空名适自误,
迫胁上楼船。
徒赐五百金,
弃之若浮烟。
辞官不受赏,
翻谪夜郎天。
夜郎万里道,
西上令人老。
扫荡六合清,
仍为负霜草。
日月无偏照,
何由诉苍昊。
良牧称神明,
深仁恤交道。
一忝青云客,
三登黄鹤楼。
顾惭祢处士,
虚对鹦鹉洲。
樊山霸气尽,
寥落天地秋。
江带峨眉雪,
川横三峡流。
万舸此中来,
连帆过扬州。
送此万里目,

旷然散我愁。
纱窗倚天开，
水树绿如发。
窥日畏衔山，
促酒喜得月。
吴娃与越艳，
窈窕夸铅红。
呼来上云梯，
含笑出帘栊。
对客小垂手，
罗衣舞春风。
宾跪请休息，
主人情未极。
览君荆山作，
江鲍堪动色。
清水出芙蓉，
天然去雕饰。
逸兴横素襟，
无时不招寻。
朱门拥虎士，
列戟何森森。
剪凿竹石开，
萦流涨清深。
登台坐水阁，
吐论多英音。
片辞贵白璧，
一诺轻黄金。
谓我不愧君，
青鸟明丹心。
五色云间鹊，
飞鸣天上来。

传闻赦书至,
却放夜郎回。
暖气变寒谷,
炎烟生死灰。
君登凤池去,
忽弃贾生才。
桀犬尚吠尧,
匈奴笑千秋。
中夜四五叹,
常为大国忧。
旌旆夹两山,
黄河当中流。
连鸡不得进,
饮马空夷犹。
安得羿善射,
一箭落妖头。

To Liangtsai Wei, Prefect of Riversummer, My Old Friend, When I Am Exiled to Nightboy at the Time of Unrest

Heaven Metropolis up there:
Twelve towers and five towns in the air.
An immortal did touch my hair
So that I could live long, for e'er.
Then I strolled to the world for fun
To finish what should have been done.
Ninety six kings in all o'er there,
Their names hung with clouds in the air.
They take sky and earth as their lot;

Warfare they have never forgot!
Now I have tried to learn kings' game,
Hoping to win honor and fame.
Howe'er, my fate has gone amiss,
I drift on, from lake to abyss.
I have learned swordsmanship in vain;
Can poem writing be a gain?
With sword mine I myself defend;
My fame for verse goes without end.
These can be nothing, just for fun;
O *Five Sighs*, from Weston I'm gone.
Just as I'm starting to leave here,
My red tassel's wet with my tear.
You are a rare talent, well-done;
Your flair o'erpowers everyone.
You set up a tent for farewell;
I'll go a hard way, rill and dell.
You see me off at the horse bower;
I'll begin my trip from this hour.
Drums or lutes can't mean what you mean;
The sun is setting to Lake Queen.
Tenth moon, I arrive in Yuchow;
The spears and halberds like stars glow.
The Lord is stranded in North Sea
While the giant whale so crazy be.
Within breaths they pass mounts and lakes,
As if Mt. Yanjan madly quakes.
The chaos I would like to quell,
And seclusion I like as well.
Sirius I would like to shoot at;
Drawing the bow, I shake like that.

Now I cry out on Golden Mound;
Where can a divine king be found?
No one the real sky horse does praise;
All in vain it gallops and neighs.
E'en if born is another Glee,
In such a state one can but flee.
In useless loneliness I frown
And I gallop here to your town.
You sit there while on you I call,
Plucking the lute in the high hall.
You are happy like saints of yore,
Hidden Spirit, Lord Mound, and more.
You have fun in Glee Hall, so pleased,
Cups and plates aligned for a feast.
Among gallants, belles and maids shine;
Before candles they stand in line.
They drink and dance like in a dream;
Their singing rings around the beam.
You play and play till early dawn,
And, satisfied, go back to town.
Ten thousand people on the way,
The camps and tents left there to stay.
We are apart, ten thousand miles,
Each having his good and bad whiles.
Cold spells and cool blows have elapsed;
And the land has almost collapsed.
The royal troops beat the Hun crowds,
Like sandstorms eclipsing the clouds.
Grass and plants shout: Lct's go and fight;
The sun and the moon lose their light.
White bones are piled up like a mound;

Why is the world in the flood drowned?
Case Dale can the empire defend;
On Han Koshu our lives depend.
Three hundred thousand troops, strong ones,
Open the gate to greet the Huns!
Peers and officials are but waste;
Loyal ones become Huns' meat paste.
The two crowns flee Capital Town;
Two capitals are falling down.
Prince E'er is ordered to command
And now he does control Ch'u Land.
Not selfish, Prince E'er would all save,
His soldiers like tigers are brave.
When people are no longer mild,
Rascals and robbers will run wild.
Only you keep Roomridge so fast;
You outshine all those in the past.
On top of Mt. Censor I rest,
Dining on mist, drinking spring blessed.
Before my door the Nine does flow,
With five lakes aligned down below.
Prince E'er's navy comes at midnight;
In Bankshine the flags wave so bright.
While I enjoy my own resource,
I'm pushed to a warship by force.
He grants me five boxes of gold;
Gold is but dirt as I behold.
His offer firmly I decline;
Exiled to Nightboy, I do whine.
Nightboy's ten thousand miles away;
There one can but age with hair gray.

The Huns wiped out, the land is clear;
But like frostbitten grass, I sear.
The sun and moon, unbiased, do glow;
How can I complain to the blue?
You are great, a prefect so kind;
You well know the folks' heart and mind.
I have been your guest, I feel shy;
Thrice I've climbed Yellow Crane so high.
What a shame, useless I remain,
Facing Parrot Shoal all in vain.
From Mt. Fan arrogance is gone;
Heaven and earth a cold hue don.
The Yangtze runs with Mt. Brow snow,
And thru the Three Gorges does flow.
Ten thousand barges do come and go;
With sails all the way to Yangchow.
Far, far I peer, standing on high,
So blankly, I relieve my sigh.
I open the window for air;
The trees ashore sprout like girls' hair.
While the sun uphill is still up,
To greet the moon, I raise my cup.
The southern girls are tall and fair;
Their fragrance does float in the air.
Some climb up a ladder, so light;
Some smile out of the shade, so bright.
They sing, waving their hands so fair,
Swaying their trains in the spring air.
They ask the guests to take a rest,
While they still enjoy them with zest.
Your verse at Mt. Chaste I've read, fine;

Chiang and Chao's flair you can outshine.
Like lilies in the clear abyss,
From nature to nature it is.
Elegance brimming in my chest,
I wait, as e'er, to be your guest.
Warriors stand in front of your door;
The halberds lined strike one with awe.
From the bamboos boulders appear;
There flows around a river clear.
In the bower with water around,
You talk fluently, what a clear sound.
Your words outweigh worth manifold;
A promise is dearer than gold.
You say I play a faithful part,
Like the blue bird with a good heart.
The five-hued magpie mid clouds flies,
Chirping all the way from the skies.
Amnesty's arrived, as is said,
But to Nightboy I'm sent instead.
The warm air falls down a vale chill;
The flaming fire goes out to nil.
You will go to Phoenix Pool there;
Do not forget your friend left here.
Do not let the Huns at us sneer,
Like Fowl Stump at High Mound did jeer.
I oft sigh a lot at midnight
For our greatest country in plight.
To the flags a mountain wind blows;
The Yellow River with waves flows.
The cocks will fight but can't get in;
The horses cower, so weak and thin.

> Where can we a King Archer find
> So as to shoot Huns e'en in blind.

* Ninety six kings: There were ninety six lords from Emperor First of Ch'in to Emperor Deepsire of T'ang.
* *O Five Sighs*: a song composed by Swan Liang, a hermit and poet of the Eastern Chin dynasty, who wrote the song to condemn the luxurious life of the upper class and convey his deep concern for the country and people.
* Weston: referring to Long Peace or Ch'ang'an if transliterated, so named because it was in West China.
* Lake Queen: a lake located in present-day Hsi'an, dug in 120 B.C. for water supply and army training.
* Yuchow: referring to an area covering present-day Peking and the north of Hopei Province.
* Mt. Yanjan: a mountain located in present-day Mongolia. It is usually used to imply an enemy with military threat.
* Golden Mound: a mound built by King Glare of Yan in order to call for talents.
* Glee: referring to Ee Yüeh, a prominent military commander. In the year of 284 B.C., he commanded the five-nation allied forces to attack the State of Ch'i and set an example of the weak overcoming the strong in war history.
* Hidden Spirit: Fuhsi if transliterated, the ancestor of Chinese and the earliest documented god of creation and king of kings in Chinese culture. Sky Water (T'ienshui) in today's Kansu Province is believed to be Hidden Spirit's birthplace, as is the topographical center of China.
* Lord Mound: Mound (2377 B.C.- 2259 B.C.), Yao if transliterated. Divine and noble, Mound has been regarded as one of Five Lords in ancient China.
* Case Dale: an ancient pass located to the east of the capital, and Lint'ao to the west.
* Han Koshu: Han Koshu (? - A.D. 757), whose surname is Koshu, of foreign extraction, a senior commander and militarist of the T'ang Empire.
* two capitals: referring to Long Peace and Loshine.
* Prince E'er: Lin Li (? - A.D. 757), the 16th son of Emperor Deepsire of T'ang. He was assigned to guard the south during Lushan An's Rebellion.
* Roomridge: a shire in the T'ang dynasty, located in present-day Hupei Province.
* Mt. Censer: a scenic peak of Mt. Lodge, looking like an incense burner.
* The Nine: the Nine Rivers, that is Bankshine or referring to the Yangtze River. As is said the river is divided into nine branches at Bankshine.

* Bankshine: an ancient name of present-day Chiuchiang, Chianghsi Province.
* magpie: a jaylike passerine corvine bird, having a long and graduated tail and featured with black-and-white coloring, which often makes loud chirps to report good news, as is believed by many Chinese.
* Nightboy: once the biggest country in the southwest existing till the Han dynasty. In 27 B.C., Nightboy, which was a provincial malarial land to Han Chinese, was wiped out by the Han and was made a county.
* Yellow Crane: referring to Yellow Crane Tower, a famous tower in Wuhan, Hupei Province.
* Parrot Shoal: a shoal located in Wuhan, Hupei Province. It is named for *Ode to the Parrot* by Scale Mi (A.D. 173 - A.D. 198), an upright man in the Three Kingdoms period. When Mi was banished to Wuhan, the magistrate gave him a parrot and required him to write a verse about it, hence *Verse to the Parrot*, comparing the parrot to himself.
* Mt. Fan: a mountain where Ch'üan Sun (A.D. 182 - A.D. 252), King of Wu in the Three Kingdoms period, made success.
* Mt. Brow: one of the four Buddhist mountains, located in Ssuch'uan Province, named for its elegant brow-shaped silhouette viewed from a distance.
* Three Gorges: referring to the three gorges of the Long River, including Big Pond Gorge, Witch Gorge, and Westridge Gorge. It implies the area around the three gorges.
* Yangchow: an important city in today's Chiangsu Province, the greatest port in China and the centre of luxury trades in the T'ang dynasty.
* Mt. Chaste: a mountain in Hupei Province, located on the west bank of the River Han. It's said to be the mountain where Ho Pian found the jade.
* Chiang: referring to Yan Chiang (A.D. 444 - A.D. 505), a statesman and litterateur through three dynasties, that is, Sung (A.D. 420 - A.D. 479), Ch'i (A.D. 479 - A.D. 502) and Liang (A.D. 502 - A.D. 557).
* Chao: referring to Chao Pao (A.D. 414 - A.D. 466), a litterateur and poet of Sung (A.D. 420 - A.D. 479) in the Southern Dynasties period.
* Phoenix Pool: implying positions of significance.
* Fowl Stump: Stump (? - 1600 B.C.), Chieh if transliterated, a tyrant and the last lord of the Hsia dynasty.
* High Mound: Lord Mound (2377 B.C.- 2259 B.C.), one of Five Lords in ancient China.
* cock: the male, usually full grown, of the domesticated fowl, having a high red crown, hence an image of a leader or champion.
* King Archer: a legendary chief in the ancient China, good at archery, who shot down the false suns that appeared in the heavens and devastated the crops.

江夏使君叔席上赠史郎中

凤凰丹禁里，
衔出紫泥书。
昔放三湘去，
今还万死馀。
仙郎久为别，
客舍问何如？
涸辙思流水，
浮云失旧居。
多惭华省贵，
不以逐臣疏。
复如竹林下，
叨陪芳宴初。
希君生羽翼，
一化北溟鱼。

To Vice Minister Shih at a Feast Hosted by My Uncle, Prefect of Riversummer

From Phoenix Palace there comes down
The edict for me to serve Crown.
To Three Hsiangs I have been exiled
And now will come back from the wild.
Away from you I have been for long;
Don't ask me how I've got along.
Fish stranded think of the abyss;
Clouds astray may their old place miss.

You don't for my case estrange me;
In your house I feel shame, you see.
It seems we've come back to the wood;
Having the feast, we feel so good.
Might you in North Sea, now I wish,
Turn into a roc from the fish!

* Riversummer: an ancient town tracing back to 350 B.C. when Sha-e was established and was officially renamed Riversummer in A.D. 589, one of the three towns that constitutes Wuhan, now called Chianghsia District under Wuhan.
* Phoenix Palace: the imperial palace or the court.
* edict: a public ordinance emanating from a sovereign and having the force of law.
* Three Hsiangs: referring to present-day Hunan Province. The Hsiang River flows into three rivers, the Li, the Cheng and the Hsiao, hence the name Three Hsiangs.
* turn into a roc: an allusion to a fable in *Sir Lush*, as reads: There in North Sea is a fish called Minnow, whose body spans about a thousand miles. When transformed into a bird, it is called Roc, whose back spans about a thousand miles.

博平郑太守自庐山千里相寻入江夏北市门见访，却之武陵，立马赠别

大梁贵公子，
气盖苍梧云。
若无三千客，
谁道信陵君。
救赵复存魏，
英威天下闻。
邯郸能屈节，
访博从毛薛。
夷门得隐沦，
而与侯生亲。
仍要鼓刀者，
乃是袖槌人。
好士不尽心，
何能保其身。
多君重然诺，
意气遥相托。
五马入市门，
金鞍照城郭。
都忘虎竹贵，
且与荷衣乐。
去去桃花源，
何时见归轩。
相思无终极，
肠断朗江猿。

An Impromptu to Prefect Cheng of Broadpeace Coming All the Way to Riversummer from Mt. Lodge and Seeing Me Off to Martial Ridge at North Market Gate

A prince you are from Greatbeam there;
Your pride overrides clouds in the air.
If three thousand guests you don't have,
Dare you claim to be Prince Way brave?
You first saved Chao and then saved Way;
Your good name travels far away.
In Hantan you fell to look tame,
And found Mao and Hsüeh from a game.
You had the hermits at the Smooth Gate
And treated Hou as your soulmate.
Don't you know the slaughterer there
Is the hero so brave, so rare?
If you love dons but don't do best,
How can you keep them so blessed?
Sir, if your promise you can keep,
We will have each other's trust deep.
You drive your cart to Market Gate,
The saddle shines to the wall, great.
You forget your prefecture high,
And get along with a low guy.
Now to Fairyland you'll depart,
When can I see your coming cart?
Our missing would go on for aye,
Grave like the river monkey's cry.

* Broadpeace: a county in today's Shantung Province.
* Riversummer: an ancient county, present-day Chianghsia District, Wuhan, Hupei Province.
* Mt. Lodge: a famous mountain with historic, cultural and religious attractions, located in present-day Chianghsi Province.
* Greatbeam: referring to the capital city of the State of Way in the Warring States period, near today's K'aifeng, Honan Province.
* Prince Way: referring to Faithridge (Hsin Ling), the youngest son of King Glare of Way, a famous militarist and statesman in the Warring States period. He was courteous to talents, attracting 3,000 hangers-on. According to historical records, he stole the military tally and commanded the troop to protect the State of Chao. As Chao and Way shared a common lot, the two states were relieved from the threat of Ch'in.
* Hantan: a city more than 3,100 years old, the capital of the State of Chao (403 B.C.- 222 B.C.) in the Eastern Chough dynasty (770 B.C.- 256 B.C.), located in present-day Hopei Province. This city was built as early as the Shang dynasty (cir. 1600 B.C.- cir. 1046 B.C.) and an imperial palace was built here for King Chow (cir. 1105 B.C.- 1046 B.C.) according to *Lonely Bamboo Annals*. The legacies and ruins in and around the town bespeak the splendor of its glorious past.
* Mao and Hsüeh: hermits who, one a gambler and the other a starch seller, became hangers-on of Prince Way because of his modesty and hospitality.
* Hou: referring to Ying Hou (? -257 B.C.), a hermit who lived as a porter of Smooth Gate of the State of Way and became a hanger-on of Prince Faithridge.

江上赠窦长史

汉求季布鲁朱家，
楚逐伍胥去章华。
万里南迁夜郎国，
三年归及长风沙。
闻道青云贵公子，
锦帆游戏西江水。
人疑天上坐楼船，
水净霞明两重绮。
相约相期何太深，
棹歌摇艇月中寻。
不同珠履三千客，
别欲论交一片心。

To T'ou, Chief of Staff When I'm on the River

Han invited Pu Chi in Chia Chu's home;
Ch'u expelled Wu from Capital to roam.
Far off I'm in Nightboy, an alien land;
Three years later I'm back to Longwind Sand.
I hear that you are the childe going high;
On the west stream a pleasure boat you ply.
All doubt high in the sky you row a boat;
Two layers of clouds on clear water float.
Getting together, how deeply you love;
You row, you sing to find the moon above.

> Three thousand guests, so differently apart,
> You can't commune or argue with your heart.

* Han: indicating Pang Liu (256 B.C.- 195 B.C.), the founding lord of Han. After he defeated Ch'u's army and won the throne, Pang Liu invited Pu Chi, former commander of Ch'u, to be an imperial guard.
* Pu Chi: once a commander of Ch'u who defeated Han's army several times. After Han won, Pu Chi hid himself and lived as a farmer for Chia Chu. With Chu's help, Pu Chi was pardoned by Pang Liu and became an imperial guard.
* Chia Chu: referring to Chia Chu of Lu, a man with justice and kind heart. In the end of the Ch'in dynasty, he helped a lot of gallants and desperate people including Pu Chi.
* Wu: referring to Tzuhsu Wu (559 B.C.- 484 B.C.), a renowned minister of Wu. In 522 B.C., Tzuhsu Wu escaped from Ch'u when his father and elder brother had been killed by King Peace.
* Nightboy: once the biggest kingdom founded by southern barbarians in the southwest existing from the Warring States period to the Han dynasty. In 27 B.C., Nightboy was wiped out by Han and was made a county.
* Longwind Sand: a shoal in the Yangtze River, located in present-day Anch'ing, Anhui Province.

赠王汉阳

天落白玉棺，
王乔辞叶县。
一去未千年，
汉阳复相见。
犹乘飞凫舄，
尚识仙人面。
鬓发何青青，
童颜皎如练。
吾曾弄海水，
清浅嗟三变。
果惬麻姑言，
时光速流电。
与君数杯酒，
可以穷欢宴。
白云归去来，
何事坐交战。

To Wang, Magistrate of Hanshine

A jade coffin falls from the skies;
Ch'iao Wang gets in and there he lies.
It's one thousand years since then;
In Hanshine I see you again.
You're still in flying wild duck shoes;
Your face like that of a fairy glows.
There, as e'er, shines your sable hair;

Your childlike cheeks like white cloth glare.
Once blue waves in the sea I played,
Sighing three changes it had made.
Just like Hemp Maid has said, indeed,
Time like lightning rushes to speed.
With you a few cups I gulp down;
At the feast in glee we may drown.
White clouds go away and come back;
Why care about richness or lack?

* Hanshine: one of the three towns in Wuhan, the present-day Hanshine District.
* Ch'iao Wang: a magistrate in the Han dynasty, who was said to have magic power. As the records say, Ch'iao went to the capital to visit the lord half a month. The lord felt strange to see him so frequently that he ordered a grand scribe to observe Chiao privately. The grand scribe found that every time Chiao arrived, there would come a pair of wild ducks. When the wild ducks had been captured, they could only find a pair of shoes. Afterwards, there was a jade coffin dropped from the sky, and Chiao thought it was Heaven's call so he got in. As he got in, the coffin closed by itself, and as the coffin was put into the grave, it buried itself.
* Hemp Maid: an alternative name of Maid Flax, a mythical figure, who looked eighteen years old but claimed to have witnessed the drying-up of East Sea for three times.

赠汉阳辅录事二首

To Secretary Fu of Hanshine, Two Poems

其 一

闻君罢官意,
我抱汉川湄。
借问久疏索,
何如听讼时?
天清江月白,
心静海鸥知。
应念投沙客,
空馀吊屈悲。

No. 1

I hear you have resigned and gone;
I sigh riv'rside, a lonely one.
May I ask: Have they different ways,
Sitting still and hearing a case?
The river clear sees the moon glow;
A serene heart the seagulls know.
I think of him who himself drowned;
Just like Yüan Chü sadly renowned.

---

* the moon: the celestial body that revolves around the earth from west to east as a satellite, which appears at night and gives off shining silvery light, an image of purity and solitude in Chinese culture.
* seagull: a kind of sea bird, any gull or large tern, a symbol of clean integrity. The seagulls in the Wordist book *Sir Line*(Liehtzu) are particularly sensitive to impurity of

motive and will make friends only with the completely guileless and disinterested.
* Yüan Ch'ü: Yüan Ch'ü (340 B.C.- 278 B.C.) is a symbol of integrity in Chinese culture. May fifth is the day when all Chinese remember this poet, a great poet of Ch'u, who threw himself into the Milo River, because he was rejected by the king and was aggrieved at his broken state.

其 二

鹦鹉洲横汉阳渡，
水引寒烟没江树。
南浦登楼不见君，
君今罢官在何处？
汉口双鱼白锦鳞，
令传尺素报情人。
其中字数无多少，
只是相思秋复春。

No. 2

Parrot Shoal lies there before Hanshine Ford;
The waves in mist are to the treetops poured.
At Southshore I climb up but can't you find;
I haven't seen you, sir, since you resigned.
I have sent twain fish with silvery scales
To tell you that my love for you ne'er fails.
Not many words I could say there inside
But my longing for you does long abide.

* Parrot Shoal: a shoal located in Wuhan, Hupei Province. It is named for *Ode to the Parrot* by Scale Mi (A.D. 173 - A.D. 198), an upright man in the Three Kingdoms period. When Mi was banished to Wuhan, the magistrate gave him a parrot and required him to write a verse about it, hence *Ode to the Parrot*, comparing the parrot to himself.
* Hanshine: one of the three towns in Wuhan, the present-day Hanshine District.
* twain fish: two fish, a symbol of a letter wherein to express one's love or missing, also the alias of a letter, because in ancient China a letter was usually written on silk and the silk was then bound in two slabs of bamboo, which were carved like a pair of fish.

江夏赠韦南陵冰

胡骄马惊沙尘起,
胡雏饮马天津水。
君为张掖近酒泉,
我窜三巴九千里。
天地再新法令宽,
夜郎迁客带霜寒。
西忆故人不可见,
东风吹梦到长安。
宁期此地忽相遇,
惊喜茫如堕烟雾。
玉箫金管喧四筵,
苦心不得申一句。
昨日绣衣倾绿樽,
病如桃李竟何言?
昔骑天子大宛马,
今乘款段诸侯门。
赖遇南平豁方寸,
复兼夫子持清论。
有似山开万里云,
四望青天解人闷。
人闷还心闷,
苦辛长苦辛。
愁来饮酒二千石,
寒灰重暖生阳春。
山公醉后能骑马,
别是风流贤主人。
头陀云月多僧气,

山水何曾称人意？
不然鸣笳按鼓戏沧流，
呼取江南女儿歌棹讴。
我且为君槌碎黄鹤楼，
君亦为吾倒却鹦鹉洲。
赤壁争雄如梦里，
且须歌舞宽离忧。

To Ice Wei, a Magistrate of Southridge, from Riversummer

The Hun warhorse, so startled, kicks up sand;
The Hun guys get a drink on Kingford strand.
You to Ope-arms arrive at Spring of Wine;
I'm exiled nine thousand miles to the line.
E'en an amnesty kind brings something new,
The exiled goes back, tinged with a frost hue.
My friend in the west I have failed to see;
The wind from east to Long Peace blows to me.
I've never expected we could meet here;
A veil of haze spreads now over our cheer.
Flutes and bands bring liveliness to the feast;
My verse cannot relieve me, not the least.
The court servant sent me brocade last night;
Who could I say like a peach in a blight?
Before, I rode a Ferghana horse great;
Now, on a nag, I cringe at a high gate.
Haply, I've met Magistrate Li so square,
And you, sir, talk with me, what a suave air!
As if all clouds have been driven away,

The blue sky above, I have a good day.
A bad mood is still a bad mood;
Those who brood continue to brood.
Moody, I'd drink two thousand pots of wine;
Broody, I hope the ash can once more shine.
Drunk, Hillman can, as ever, his horse ride;
With his guests, he would throw all cares aside.
Mendicant Fane offers much Buddhist air;
Could hills and rills like this please humans e'er?
Or else I'll play the flute, beat the drum and the water pour,
And more, call the southern sons and daughters to ply their oar.
For you Yellow Crane Tower I'll throw my fist out to break;
For me you'll pull out all your power to Parrot Shoal shake.
Like a dream is the bloody Red Wall war;
Now do drink and dance to discharge our sore.

* Riversummer: an ancient county, present-day Chianghsia District, Wuhan, Hupei Province.
* Kingford Bridge: a bridge of great importance in Loshine, which connected two prosperous blocks of the ancient city.
* Ope-arms: Changyeh if transliterated, a prefectural city, one of the four garrison cities built by Emperor Martial of Han (156 B.C.- 87 B.C.), located in present-day Kansu Province. It is a town of importance on the Silk Road, named for the wish to "open arms to the west".
* Spring of Wine: Chiuch'üan if transliterated, a prefectural city, built by Emperor Martial of Han (156 B.C.- 87 B.C.) to garrison the border, located in present-day Kansu Province. It is a town of importance on the Silk Road, as is said to have possessed a natural fountain of wine.
* Long Peace: Ch'ang'an if transliterated, the metropolis of gold, the capital of the T'ang, the largest city in the world then, with a population of one million. As the starting point of the Silk Road and the birthplace of Chinese civilization, it has been a capital for thirteen dynasties, enjoying the privilege of the Museum of Chinese History, and it is now the capital of Sha'anhsi Province.
* Ferghana horse: Ferghana was an ancient state existing in Ferghana Basin. According

to historical records, the horses from Ferghana are a precious kind. As it sprints, its shoulders swell and it sweats like bleeding.
* Magistrate Li: referring to Chiyao Li, a cousin from the poet's family, who was a magistrate of Southpeace.
* Hillman: referring to the fifth son of T'ao Shan, one of the Seven Sages of the Bamboo Grove in the Chin dynasty. He was gentle and graceful as his father. When he was an official, the nation was falling apart and other officials were worried and depressed. Hillman, however, lived a casual life. Every time he hanged out, he would hold a banquet and get drunk at the High Sun Pool.
* Mendicant Fane: an ancient fane roughly located in Hupei Province.
* Yellow Crane Tower: a famous ancient tower built in the Three Kingdoms period, in present-day Wuhan, Hupei Province.
* Parrot Shoal: a shoal located in Wuhan, Hupei Province. It is named for *Ode to the Parrot* by Scale Mi (A.D. 173 – A.D. 198), an upright man in the Three Kingdoms period. When Mi was banished to Wuhan, the magistrate gave him a parrot and required him to write a verse about it, hence *Ode to the Parrot*, comparing the parrot to himself.
* Red Wall: In the year of A.D. 208, Ch'üan Sun and Pei Liu fought against Ts'ao Ts'ao at Red Wall. Ch'üan Sun's general, Yü Chou, burnt Ts'ao's army by feigning surrender.

赠 卢 司 户

秋色无远近，
出门尽寒山。
白云遥相识，
待我苍梧间。
借问卢耽鹤，
西飞几岁还？

To Lu, a Household Registrar

Fall mist not near or far, no less or more,
All chill mountains out of the door.
The white cloud knowing the fresh breeze
Waits for me between phoenix trees.
May I ask you, o westbound crane,
To fly back and see me again?

* westbound crane: referring to Pai Li's friend Registrar Lu. It is an allusion to a myth that a hermit having the same family name as Lu changed into a crane according to *Notes on Rivers*, an old Chinese geography book.

赠从弟南平太守之遥二首
To Chihyao Li, My Cousin, Magistrate of Southpeace, Two Poems

其 一

少年不得意，
落拓无安居。
愿随任公子，
欲钓吞舟鱼。
常时饮酒逐风景，
壮心遂与功名疏。
兰生谷底人不锄，
云在高山空卷舒。
汉家天子驰驷马，
赤军蜀道迎相如。
天门九重谒圣人，
龙颜一解四海春。
彤庭左右呼万岁，
拜贺明主收沉沦。
翰林秉笔回英眄，
麟阁峥嵘谁可见？
承恩初入银台门，
著书独在金銮殿。
龙驹雕镫白玉鞍，
象床绮食黄金盘。
当时笑我微贱者，
却来请谒为交欢。
一朝谢病游江海，

畴昔相知几人在？
前门长揖后门关，
今日结交明日改。
爱君山岳心不移，
随君云雾迷所为。
梦得池塘生春草，
使我长价登楼诗。
别后遥传临海作，
可见羊何共和之。

No. 1

I, a young man, so down and out,
Doing nothing, loafing about.
Prince Jen, to follow you I wish
With a hook to catch a giant fish.
Helpless, I just drink and in hostels play;
No ambition, no fame or rank will stay!
Orchids down a dale no one will sustain;
Clouds over a mountain just float in vain.
Suddenly, His Majesty sends His men
To fetch me like welcoming Ssuma then.
I go through nine gates to worship the crown;
His broad smile like a breeze dispels all frown.
Long live Your Majesty, all shout in the hall
To thank Lord for saving one from a fall.
In Brushwood I write to draw the Lord's eyes;
In all splendor here who will see me rise?
By Silver Gate I have His grace so bright;
In Golden Hall I write fast with delight.
Sky horse, carved stirrups and saddle of jade;

Good food, Ivory bed, gold plates and brocade.
Those who have jeered at me as so abased
Come to pay homage, hoping to be raised.
Once I'm down and float to river and sea,
Who of those guys would accompany me?
Greeting me with smiles, then slapping the door,
They change quickly, and I have friends no more.
I love you because you stand fast, stand true;
I would follow you, whatever you do.
I would dream of verse writing in spring breeze
So I could climb high and my price increase.
I'd send you my verse after our good bye;
Someone, I'm sure, will write verse in reply.

* Southpeace: referring to present-day Ch'ungch'ing.
* Prince Jen: a legendary figure recorded in *Sir Lush*. Prince Jen was good at fishing. He fished at East Sea with a huge hook and fifty bulls. Having been waiting on Mt. Summit for a year, he did not get any. Not long after, he caught a fish big enough to feed the people from Chechiang to Mt. Green Tree. Prince Jen, lofty and broadminded, has been regarded as a supramundane figure in Chinese literature.
* orchid: a terrestrial or epiphytic monocotyledonous plant, one of the four most important floral images in Chinese literature, which are wintersweet, orchid, bamboo, and chrysanthemum.
* Ssuma: Hsiangju Ssuma (179 B.C.- 118 B.C.), a representative verse writer in Chinese literary history.
* Brushwood: formally known as Brushwood Academy, an imperial academy for literature and arts. Pai Li was once appointed to serve in Brushwood as Emperor Deepsire appreciated his talent.
* Silver Gate: a palace gate close to Brushwood Academy.
* sky horse: According to historical records, the sky horse from Kusana is a precious kind. As it sprints, its shoulders swell and it sweats as if bleeding.

其 二

东平与南平，
今古两步兵。
素心爱美酒，
不是顾专城。
谪官桃源去，
寻花几处行？
秦人如旧识，
出户笑相迎。

No. 2

He was east there, you are south here,
You two, one for wine, one for cheer.
In all wine mellow you would drown,
Not caring your post of the town.
Demoted, you go down your tower
To stroll places to find your flower.
If Ch'in folks know you as before,
They will greet you out of their door.

* Ch'in folks: According to Poolbright T'ao's writing, a group of Ch'in people fled to Peach Blossom Source to keep away from the turbulent days, and the people and their offsprings had lived an idyllic and isolated life for 500 years before a fisherman of Chin stumbled into the village.

赠潘侍御论钱少阳

绣衣柱史何昂藏,
铁冠白笔横秋霜。
三军论事多引纳,
阶前虎士罗干将。
虽无二十五老者,
且有一翁钱少阳。
眉如松雪齐四皓,
调笑可以安储皇。
君能礼此最下士,
九州拭目瞻清光。

To P'an, the Royal Censor, an Evaluation of Firstshine Ch'ien

The censor in silk looks so great and grand;
With your white brush, you sweep frost off the land.
For strategies, the troops consult your mind,
Guards and fighters before the steps aligned.
Though no twenty five saints sit in the hall,
There's an oldster, Firstshine Ch'ien you may call.
With his brows like snow and his hair so white,
He can safeguard the crown with a smile bright.
Sir, since you respect an old man so low,
All the world look up to you for your glow.

* censor in silk: referring to a royal or imperial censor, normally clad in silk, a third-

grade government official.
* silk: the fine, soft, shiny fiber produced by silk worms to form their cocoons, and the thread or fabric made from this fibre is used as material for clothing. And it can be any clothing made of silk.
* brush: any of various writing brushes or called Chinese brushes, widely used in Chinese history, invented or renovated by Tien Meng (259 B.C.- 210 B.C.), a general in the Ch'in dynasty.
* twenty five saints: a think tank.
* Firstshine Ch'ien: unidentified. We only know that he was one of the twenty five saints mentioned by Pai Li.

赠柳圆

竹实满秋浦，
凤来何苦饥。
还同月下鹊，
三绕未安枝。
夫子即琼树，
倾柯拂羽仪。
怀君恋明德，
归去日相思。

To Yüan Liu

Autumn Shore sees fruit of bamboo;
Why does Phoenix in hunger coo?
And the magpie neath the moon there,
To perch, it, circling, finds nowhere.
Sir, you are a nectar tree fair,
Drooping your branches to show care.
I worship your virtue and grace,
Missing you nights, missing you days.

* Autumn Shore: a county of T'ang, 40 kilometers southwest of Poolton in today's Anhui Province, teeming with flora and fauna and rich in silver and copper resources.
* phoenix: a legendary bird of great beauty, unique of its kind, which was supposed to live five or six hundred years before consuming itself by fire, rising again from its ashes to live through another cycle, a symbol of immortality. In Chinese mythology, the phoenix only perches on phoenix trees, i.e. firmiana, only eats firmiana fruit, and only drinks sweet spring water, and this mythic bird appears only in times of peace and

sagacious rule.
* magpie: a jaylike passerine corvine bird, having a long and graduated tail and featured with black-and-white coloring, which often makes loud chirps to report good news, as is believed by many Chinese.
* nectar tree: a fairy tree in Chinese mythology, which is twenty thousand meters tall and three hundred meters in circumference, often used as a metaphor for saintly people or beauties.

流夜郎半道承恩放还兼欣克复之美书怀示息秀才

黄口为人罗,
白龙乃鱼服。
得罪岂怨天,
以愚陷网目。
鲸鲵未翦灭,
豺狼屡翻覆。
悲作楚地囚,
何日秦庭哭。
遭逢二明主,
前后两迁逐。
去国愁夜郎,
投身窜荒谷。
半道雪屯蒙,
旷如鸟出笼。
遥欣克复美,
光武安可同。
天子巡剑阁,
储皇守扶风。
扬袂正北辰,
开襟揽群雄。
胡兵出月窟,
雷破关之东。
左扫因右拂,
旋收洛阳宫。
回舆入咸京,
席卷六合通。

叱咤开帝业，
手成天地功。
大驾还长安，
两日忽再中。
一朝让宝位，
剑玺传无穷。
愧无秋毫力，
谁念矍铄翁。
弋者何所慕，
高飞仰冥鸿。
弃剑学丹砂，
临炉双玉童。
寄言息夫子，
岁晚陟方蓬。

To Hsi, a Showcharm, When I'm Set Free on My Way to Nightboy and Hear of the Restoration

Brown sparrows are prone to be caught;
White dragons are bent to be shot.
How can we of Heaven complain?
We are trapped as we are insane.
The whales have not yet been wiped out;
The wolves jump up again to shout.
A prisoner in Ch'u, I sadly sigh;
When could I at the Ch'in court cry?
Haply, we have two crowns so wise,
Although I have been expelled twice.
To Nightboy I've run a long way;

Exiled, in the wilderness I stay.
An amnesty comes on the way;
A bird out of the cage, hurray!
Our land afar restored, rare glare!
How can Lightmight's success compare?
Sword Pavilion our Lord patrols;
And Fufeng our crown prince controls.
Important positions we have,
And welcome are all heroes brave.
The Hun soldiers come from Moon Den
And break thru the pass to East then.
Sweeping and mopping up and down,
The royal troops restore Loshine Town.
Lord's carts come back to Capital,
Having cleared the six bounds for all.
With hails gained is imperial worth;
A success for Heaven and earth.
The royals come back to abide;
The two suns sit there side by side.
Deepsire now demises his throne;
The seal and sceptre are passed on.
I've spent no efforts I feel shame;
I am remembered all the same.
What does a good archer admire?
Wild geese that fly above and higher.
I throw my sword for cinnabar;
By the furnace two fairies are.
O Teacher, please listen to me,
Old, in Fairyland I'd like to be.

---

* Nightboy: once the biggest country in the southwest of China, existing till the Han

dynasty, which was a malarial land to Han Chinese. In 27 B.C., Nightboy was wiped out by the Han and was made a county.

* Brown sparrows: referring to young sparrows whose beaks are still brown. Grown sparrows are not easy to be caught for they are usually cautious, but young sparrows are easy to be trapped for greediness.
* White dragons are bent to be shot: an allusion to the remonstrance of Tzuhsu Wu, a renowned minister of Wu. Tsehsu Wu told a story that a white dragon lost its eye because it was disguised as a fish.
* the State of Ch'u: a vassal state of Chough, one of the powers in the Warring States period, conquered and annexed by Ch'in in 223 B.C.
* Lightmight: referring to Hsiu Liu (6 B.C. - A.D. 57), who re-established the governance of Han and started the reign of the Eastern Han.
* Sword Pavilion: a strategic pass with a plank road built along cliffs in present-day Ssuch'uan Province.
* Fufeng: a county in Sha'anhsi.
* Moon Den: referring to the extreme western land.
* Deepsire: referring to Hsuan Tsung the emperor (A.D. 685 - A.D. 762), the ninth emperor of the T'ang dynasty. When a prince, he was regarded as wise and valiant, a sportsman accomplished in all knightly exercises and a master of all elegant arts. He established Pear Garden, an operatic school, where actors and actresses were trained, and the prototype of the modern Chinese drama was developed. Under his enthusiastic patronage, arts and letters flourished. Indeed, his reign is often considered the pinnacle of Chinese cultural achievement.
* wild goose: an undomesticated goose that is caring and responsible, taken as a symbol of benevolence, righteousness, good manner, wisdom and faith in Chinese culture.
* Fairyland: an imaginary ideal abode for immortals, sometimes thought of as being in the middle of East Sea, sometimes high above in the sky.

赠张相镐
To Premier Hao Chang

其 一

神器难窃弄,
天狼窥紫宸。
六龙迁白日,
四海暗胡尘。
昊穹降元宰,
君子方经纶。
澹然养浩气,
欻起持大钧。
秀骨象山岳,
英谋合鬼神。
佐汉解鸿门,
生唐为后身。
拥旄秉金钺,
伐鼓乘朱轮。
虎将如雷霆,
总戎向东巡。
诸侯拜马首,
猛士骑鲸鳞。
泽被鱼鸟悦,
令行草木春。
圣智不失时,
建功及良辰。
丑虏安足纪,
可贻幪与巾。

倒泻溟海珠，
尽为入幕珍。
冯异献赤伏，
邓生倏来臻。
庶同昆阳举，
再睹汉仪新。
昔为管将鲍，
中奔吴隔秦。
一生欲报主，
百代思荣亲。
其事竟不就，
哀哉难重陈。
卧病宿松山，
苍茫空四邻。
风云激壮志，
枯槁惊常伦。
闻君自天来，
目张气益振。
亚夫得剧孟，
敌国空无人。
扪虱对桓公，
愿得论悲辛。
大块方噫气，
何辞鼓青蘋。
斯言倘不合，
归老汉江滨。

No. 1

The sceptre is not to be played;
To seize the throne, tries Sirus made.

Six dragons move on to the sun;
The four seas are dimmed by the Hun.
Heaven sends the premier to earth,
Who is learned and just with worth.
In great aptitude he does stand;
And the state power he keeps in hand.
Like a high mountain he does tower;
His talents make all demons cower.
Like Liang Chang sparkling at Swan Gate,
Of T'ang you are the pillar great.
Hatchets, spears and axes held high,
Red carts drawn by white steeds run by.
Like thunder the marshal does roar
And commands his troops east to war.
Before your horse vassal lords bow;
Your brave men look powerful enow.
Your grace sees fish jump and birds sing;
Your order greets a lively spring.
As our divine Lord is in power;
You seize the day, seize the hour.
The ugly foe you needn't care;
You can send him a woman's wear.
Your aides are pearls with a bright hue;
All the pearls now sparkle for you.
Ee Feng proffers you a red sign;
Yü Teng comes as you are divine.
You'll save Queenshine out of the bane;
We'll witness Han's splendor again.
Like Kuan and Pao we've the same heart,
Although you're north, I'm south, apart.
I'd like to repay our Lord's grace,

So we could our ancestors praise.
What I would do has not begun;
So miserable, what could be done?
I lodge on Pine Mound, lying ill;
No neighbors, so void is the hill.
The wind and clouds do me inspire;
But I age fast, in a state dire.
I hear you've been sent from the sky;
In high spirit, I'd have a try.
Yafu got Chümeng brave and live,
So no enemy could survive.
Like Meng's talk to Lord Huan did glow,
I'd like to share with you my woe.
The nature gives rise to a breeze,
Which you can see from duckweeds.
If what I say fits not your heart;
To rivers and lakes I'll depart.

* Sirus: referring to Lushan An who rebelled against the House of T'ang. Sirus in Chinese astrology represents invasion.
* the Hun: referring to Lushan An, who was of the Kitan race, who distinguished himself in fighting against his own tribes, won the favor of Jade Ring and the confidence of Emperor Deepsire. His promotion being rapid, he was ennobled as a count, and made the governor of the border provinces of the north, where he held under command the best armies of the empire and nursed an inordinate ambition to own the empire.
* Liang Chang (250 B.C.- 186 B.C.): a prominent statesman and counsellor, and one of the founders of Han. He retired from the center of power as the House of Han was consolidated.
* Swan Gate: referring to the outskirt of Allshine, where Yü Hsiang (232 B.C.- 202 B.C.), Overlord of West Ch'u, held a banquet with the intention of murdering Pang Liu (256 B.C.- 195 B.C.), the founding lord of the Han dynasty. With Liang Chang's help, Pang Liu escaped, which is considered to have an indirect impact on the Ch'u-Han war.

Ever since then, Swan Gate has been used to indicate banquets that harbor malicious intentions.
* T'ang: the T'ang dynasty (A.D. 618 - A.D. 907) or the T'ang Empire. The three hundred years of the T'ang dynasty witnessed a most brilliant era of national power, culture and refinement, unsurpassed in all the annals of China, the Middle Kingdom.
* pearl: a lustrous, calcareous concretion deposited in layers around a central nucleus in the shells of various mollusks, and largely used as a gem.
* Ee Feng: Ee Feng (? - A.D. 34), one of the founding commanders of the Eastern Han. He interpreted it as an auspicious sign when Lord Lightmight dreamed of riding a red dragon.
* Yü Teng: Yü Teng (A.D. 2 - A.D. 58), one of the founding commanders of the Eastern Han.
* Queenshine: an ancient town in present-day Honan Province, where Hsiu Liu won his decisive battle.
* Kuan and Pao: referring to Chung Kuan (723 B.C.- 645 B.C.) and Shuya Pao (? - 644 B.C.), statesmen and ministers of Chi, and true friends to each other.
* Pine Mound: what is today's Lodging Pines (Susung) in today's Anhui Province. Sleeping Pines is a name changed from Pine Mound because Pai Li lodged there when ill.
* Yafu: referring to Yafu Chou (199 B.C.- 143 B.C.), a general of great reputation in the Han dynasty, who once felt relieved when hearing that Chümeng did not fight against him.
* Chümeng: a gallant in the Fore-Ch'in period, who often saved people from danger.
* Meng: referring to Meng Wang (A.D. 325 - A.D. 375), a renowned strategist and statesman in the Eastern Chin dynasty. As he talked with Lord Huan, he removed lice as if there was nothing wrong, showing a liberal attitude instead of being punctilious.
* Lord Huan: referring to Wen Huan (A.D. 312 - A.D. 373), a military strategist and statesman in the Eastern Chin dynasty.

其 二

本家陇西人，
先为汉边将。
功略盖天地，
名飞青云上。
苦战竟不侯，
富年颇惆怅。
世传崆峒勇，
气激金风壮。
英烈遗厥孙，
百代神犹王。
十五观奇书，
作赋凌相如。
龙颜惠殊宠，
麟阁凭天居。
晚途未云已，
蹭蹬遭谗毁。
想像晋末时，
崩腾胡尘起。
衣冠陷锋镝，
戎虏盈朝市。
石勒窥神州，
刘聪劫天子。
抚剑夜吟啸，
雄心日千里。
誓欲斩鲸鲵，
澄清洛阳水。
六合洒霖雨，
万物无凋枯。

我挥一杯水，
自笑何区区。
因人耻成事，
贵欲决良图。
灭虏不言功，
飘然陟蓬壶。
惟有安期舄，
留之沧海隅。

No. 2

By origin, I am a West Bulge man,
Going back to Broad Li in Han.
His merits shine on earth and sky;
His fame reaches the clouds on high.
No dukedom on him was conferred;
In his prime his sighs could be heard.
Those from Mt. Hollow are so bold
That their pride shakes the sky, as told.
Kuang's spirit was passed to his sons,
Who for decades have been brave ones.
At fifteen I read a great book;
For my prose Ssuma had to look.
I once won His Majesty's grace;
Unicorn Tower did me amaze.
So thwarted in my later years;
I did incur slanders and sneers.
It's so like the last years of Chin,
The Hun dust whirling with much din.
Rich men sway their swords up and down;
The Huns swarm in the court and town.

Like Shih, the chief, o'erlooks the land;
Like Liu, the thief, keeps Lord in hand.
I oft howl with my sword at night;
I'd rush to the Huns and them fight.
I would kill the whales I do swear
So the Lo River could be clear.
I would splash rain to the whole land
So all the plants can firmly stand.
A cup of wine aground I splash
And jeer at myself: why so rash?
On others I hate to depend,
I need have a good plan and end.
When I have finished the Hun foe,
To Fairyland there I would go.
Just like Ch'i An, the saint, before,
I would leave my jade shoes ashore.

* West Bulge: an ancient shire located in present-day Kansu Province, the birthplace of General Broad Li or Kuang Li if transliterated.
* Mt. Hollow: a mountain in present-day Kansu Province, famous for martial arts. As is said, people here are brave and skillful at fighting battles. And it is a Wordist sanctuary, where Lord Yellow learned the Word from Sir Goodharvest. *Sir Lush* keeps a record of this inquiry, as reads: Lord Yellow had reigned nineteen years and his orders were carried out all over the land. Having heard that Sir Goodharvest lived on Mt. Hollow, he went to pay him a visit, saying: "I hear that you know the very Word. May I inquire of you about the quintessence of the very Word? I would acquire the essence of Heaven and earth to help five grains and sustain my people. And I also want to govern Shade and Shine so that all things may grow well." Because of this event, Mt. Hollow is esteemed as the first Wordist mountain in China.
* Kuang: referring to Broad Li (? - 119 B.C.), Kuang Li if transliterated, a renowned general fighting against the Huns in the Han dynasty, called Flying General by the Huns.
* Ssuma: Hsiangju Ssuma (179 B.C.- 118 B.C.) in full name, a talented litterateur in the

Han dynasty, a representative verse writer in Chinese literary history.
* Unicorn Tower: also known as Unicorn Mound, built in the Han dynasty to memorize those who made great contributions to the empire.
* Shih: referring to Le Shih (A.D. 274 – A.D. 333), a chief of northerners called Rams, who took over a large part of the northern land in A.D. 329 and established his kingdom, Chao (A.D. 319 – A.D. 352).
* Liu: referring to Ts'ung Liu (? – A.D. 318), a chief of Hun origin, who provoked political chaos by attacking Loshine and Long Peace, and capturing and killing the lords, and ended the reign of the Western Chin dynasty.
* Ch'i An: an immortal who had sold medicine at the seaside of East Sea for a thousand years. Emperor First of Ch'in once talked with him for three days. What he talked about was so profound that the emperor could not understand. The emperor gave him a great deal of gold. An Chi left the gold at Fuhsiang Pavilion with a letter to ask the emperor to visit him on Fairy Sea a thousand years later.

闻谢杨儿吟猛虎词,因此有赠

同州隔秋浦,
闻吟猛虎词。
晨朝来借问,
知是谢杨儿。

Hearing Yang'er Hsieh Singing A Tiger, Hence the Poem

Across Autumn Shore o'er there
Someone sings *A Tiger* I hear.
I ask who is in the dawn breeze;
He replies Hsieh Yang'er it is.

* Autumn Shore: a county of T'ang, 40 kilometers southwest of Poolton in today's Anhui Province, teeming with flora and fauna and rich in silver and copper resources.
* *A Tiger*: a poem composed Kuanghsi Ch'u (cir. A.D. 706 - A.D. 763), a T'ang poet. A tiger, a large carnivorous feline mammal is praised as king of all animals in Chinese culture.

宿清溪主人

夜到清溪宿，
主人碧岩里。
檐楹挂星斗，
枕席响风水。
月落西山时，
啾啾夜猿起。

In Blue Stream I Stay

In Blue Stream I stay for the night;
My host's house is on Rocky Height.
Stars shine to the eaves overhead;
Wind and water sound to my bed.
The moon sets to the western hills,
Wherein one can hear monkeys' shrills.

* Blue Stream: a place named after a stream that originated in Mt. Nine Flora in Anhui Province.
* Rocky Height: a steep and rocky mountain near Blue Stream.
* the moon: the planet of the earth, which appears at night and gives off shining silvery light, an image of purity and solitude in Chinese culture.
* monkey: any of a group of primates having elongate limbs, hands and feet adapted for grasping, and a highly developed nervous system, including marmosets, baboons, and macaques, but not the anthropoid apes, though monkeys and apes are used alternatively in Chinese.

系寻阳上崔相涣三首
To Premier Ts'ui in Bankshine, Three Poems

其 一

邯郸四十万，
同日陷长平。
能回造化笔，
或冀一人生。

No. 1

Four hundred thousand from Hantan
Fell flat in Long Calm in one day.
One may come back to life, perhaps,
If the Creator's brush you could sway.

* Bankshine: an ancient name of present-day Chiuchiang, Chianghsi Province.
* Long Calm: an ancient town of Chao, where the Ch'in troops led by Rise White (Ch'i Pai) (? - 257 B.C.) wiped out four hundred thousand Chao soldiers and buried them alive in 260 B.C.

其 二

毛遂不堕井，
曾参宁杀人。
虚言误公子，
投杼惑慈亲。
白璧双明月，
方知一玉真。

No. 2

Sui Mao did not to the well fall;
Sen Tseng did not kill one at all.
Fables and tales destroy a name;
A mother may flee all the same.
If a jade disc is double bright,
One may know it is purely white.

* Sui Mao: Sui Mao (285 B.C.- 228 B.C.), a lobbyist from Chao who recommended himself to visit Ch'u and gained his fame by making an alliance between Ch'u and Chao. "Sui Mao fell to the well" indicates a rumour. It's said that there was a man called Sui Mao who fell into a well and got drowned, and when the lord mourned for his death, he found the Mao in the well was not the Mao in his think tank.
* Sen Tseng: Sen Tseng (505 B. C. - 435 B. C.), one of Confucius' students, a representative of Confucianism. "Sen Tseng killed someone" also indicates a rumour. It's said a man who had the same name as Tseng killed a person. Others told that Confucius's mother that Tseng committed murder, but his mother did not believe it. As the mother was told the third time, she vacillated over the rumour.
* jade discs: jewels worn by royal families and nobles. Jade is exclusive to the upper echelon of the society, but gold and silver are not, as a saying goes, "Gold is priced while jade is priceless."

其 三

虚传一片雨，
枉作阳台神。
纵为梦里相随去，
不是襄王倾国人。

No. 3

If falsely you predict a rain,
You're Goddess on Sun Mound in vain.
Even if in your dream she treats you well,
She's not a royal beauty, not the belle.

* Sun Mound: the place where Goddess of Mt. Witch stays, implying a place where lovers may date.
* she: referring to Goddess of Mt. Witch, a beautiful fairy dwelling in Mt. Witch, who shaped herself as clouds at dawn and turned into rain at dusk. In myths, King Huai of Ch'u once met her in his dream, and had an intercourse overnight. The story was recorded by Jade Sung, a student of Yüan Ch'ü's, when he travelled to Cloud Dream Moor with King Hsiang.

巴陵赠贾舍人

贾生西望忆京华,
湘浦南迁莫怨嗟。
圣主恩深汉文帝,
怜君不遣到长沙。

To Secretary Chia at Paridge

You look west to see Capital so high;
While moving to South Shore, please do not sigh.
His grace outweighs Lord Civil's favor grand
That you are dispatched afar to Long Sand.

* Secretary Chia: referring to Chih Chia (A.D. 718 - A.D. 772), a poet and official who met Pai Li at Paridge after being degraded.
* Paridge: the ancient name of Yüehshine, where Emperor Civil of Han was buried.
* you: referring to Ee Chia, a political commentator and litterateur in the Western Han dynasty, who gained his fame when he was young. When he served as an official, he was envied by those higher-ranking ministers and the lord sent him away to Long Sand.
* Lord Civil: referring to Emperor Civil of Han.
* Long Sand: Ch'angsha if transliterated, a remote place away from the capital in ancient China.

古近体诗二十五首
Old-new Rhythmic Poetry, 25 Poems

赠别舍人弟台卿之江南

去国客行远，
还山秋梦长。
梧桐落金井，
一叶飞银床。
觉罢揽明镜，
鬓毛飒已霜。
良图委蔓草，
古貌成枯桑。
欲道心下事，
时人疑夜光。
因为洞庭叶，
飘落之潇湘。
令弟经济士，
谪居我何伤。
潜虬隐尺水，
著论谈兴亡。
客遇王子乔，
口传不死方。
入洞过天地，
登真朝玉皇。
吾将抚尔背，
挥手遂翱翔。

Seeing Off Brother, Secretary T'aich'ing to South

From homeland you're going away;
For your return in my dream I pray.
Phoenix tree leaves to the well fall;
One flies to the bed through the hall.
I wake up, and my mirror bright
Shows me my hair is turning white.
My plans have been to thistles thrown;
My face has been like dry leaves blown.
What I think of I would speak out;
But a bright pearl may cause a doubt.
The fallen leaves from Lake Cavehall
Will fly to the Hsiang and there fall.
You're who where the state can rely;
Your demotion there makes me sigh.
A dragon that in a trench lies
Can only dream of fall and rise.
I've met Front, the immortal sage,
Who teaches the way not to age.
I wish in Fairy Cave I stayed
And went to worship Lord of Jade.
Now your back I stroke and stroke more;
Then farewell, to free clouds I'll soar.

* thistle: any of various plants of the composite family, with prickly leaves and heads of white, purple, pink, or yellow flowers.
* pearl: a smooth, lustrous, usually white and bluish-gray, calcareous concretion

deposited in layers around a central nucleus in the shells of various mollusks or oysters, and largely used as a gem, medicine or given as a gift, a metaphor for the dearest one, a representation of nobility, purity and dignity in Chinese culture.
* Lake Cavehall: a large lake in Hunan Province.
* Hsiang: referring to present-day Hunan Province.
* dragon: Though variously understood as a large reptile, a marine monster, a jackal and so on in Western culture, it has been esteemed as a fabulous serpent-like giant winged animal, which can change its girth and length, a totem of the Chinese nation, a symbol of benevolence and sovereignty in Chinese culture.
* Front: referring to Prince of Front (567 B.C.– 549 B.C.), the first son of King Spirit of Chough. He was an intelligent and courageous young man. Though high as a prince, he had few desires and was keen on the Word. As legend goes, after his early death he, riding a white crane, rose to the sky and became immortal.
* Lord of Jade: the deity of highest power in Chinese mythology, identifiable with the Word or God in western culture for having the same attributes as omnipresence, omniscience and omnipotence and being personal as the ultimate sovereign of all, living and non-living.

醉后赠王历阳

书秃千兔毫，
诗裁两牛腰。
笔踪起龙虎，
舞袖拂云霄。
双歌二胡姬，
更奏远清朝。
举酒挑朔雪，
从君不相饶。

To Wang, Magistrate of Leeshine after I'm Drunk

I've used hare hair, ten carts of packs;
And written scrolls, two cattle racks.
My brush runs thru, live and loud;
My sleeve waves up to the white cloud.
Two Hun girls sing a duet song
From deep night until early dawn.
You urge me to drink in the snow;
When you drink, I ne'er reply slow.

* hare hair: hair of a hare, a rodent (genus *Lepus*) with cleft upper lip, long ears, and long hind legs, characterized by its timidity and swiftness, habitating woodland, farmland or grassland.
* Leeshine: an ancient town of strategic importance, in present-day Ho County, Anhui Province. It is the hub of roads and waterways between the Long River and the Huai River, with a rich historic legacy such as Soul Shrine of Overlord Yü Hsiang and Yün

Wu's Lane, Yarn Washer's Shrine and so on.
* Hun girls: foreign girls from west or north of China, often selling wine in wine shops in the T'ang dynasty.

赠历阳褚司马，时此公为稚子舞，故作是诗也

北堂千万寿，
侍奉有光辉。
先同稚子舞，
更著老莱衣。
因为小儿啼，
醉倒月下归。
人间无此乐，
此乐世中稀。

To Ssuma Ch'u in Leeshine, Who Dances a Child's Dance, Hence My Poem

In North Hall your old parents stay;
You wait on them with a bright ray.
In gay clothes, dancing like a child,
You amuse them to be beguiled.
You play a child that sobs and cries,
And one who, moonlit, so drunk lies.
In this world there's no such pleasure;
Such pleasure here is a treasure.

* Leeshine: an ancient town of strategic importance, tracing back to the Spring and Autumn period, in present-day Ho County, Anhui Province. It is the hub of roads and waterways between the Long River and the Huai River, with a rich historic legacy such as Soul Shrine of Overlord Yü Hsiang and Yün Wu's Lane, Yarn Washer's Shrine and so on.

* In gay clothes, dancing like a child: an allusion to Sir Laolai (cir. 599 B.C.- 479 B.C.), a Wordist thinker in the Late Spring and Autumn period. As is said, Sir Laolai, very kind to his parents, often played a baby in colored gay clothes to amuse them.

对雪醉后赠王历阳

有身莫犯飞龙鳞,
有手莫辨猛虎须。
君看昔日汝南市,
白头仙人隐玉壶。
子猷闻风动窗竹,
相邀共醉杯中绿。
历阳何异山阴时,
白雪飞花乱人目。
君家有酒我何愁?
客多乐酣秉烛游。
谢尚自能鸲鹆舞,
相如免脱鹔鹴裘。
清晨鼓棹过江去,
千里相思明月楼。

To Magistrate Wang of Leeshine When I'm Drunk in Snow

Don't stroke athwart a flying dragon's scale;
Don't pull aside a fiery tiger's tail.
Yesterday's Junan Market don't you see?
In the jade pot hid a gray-haired fairy.
Tsuyu heard wind blow bamboo by the sill
And was asked to share a cup of green fill.
Now you are so smart, just like Tsuyu then,
While snowflakes fly about to dazzle men.

What worries do I have if you have wine?
We'll hold a candle to play just as fine.
An Hsieh can dance for his mynah bird play;
Ssuma need not doff his Phoenix Array.
At dawn I'll go across, plying the oar;
Atop the moonlit tower I'll miss you more.

* Leeshine: an ancient town of strategic importance, in present-day Ho County, Anhui Province, at the hub of roads and waterways between the Long River and the Huai River. It boasts a rich historic legacy such as Soul Shrine of Overlord Yü Hsiang and Yün Wu's Lane, Yarn Washer's Shrine and so on.
* jade pot: referring to the pure world of immortality, where elixirs are concocted, and in some other cases alluding to the purity of the holder's heart.
* Tsuyu: referring to Huichi Wang (A.D. 338 – A.D. 386), a renowned calligrapher with a carefree attitude in the Eastern Chin dynasty.
* candle: a cylinder of tallow, wax, or other solid fat, containing a wick, to give light when burning, first seen in literature in the Eastern Han dynasty. The most famous lines about candles are from a poem by a T'ang poet named Shangyin Li, "Silkworms stop offering silk when they die; / Candles become ash as their tears run dry."
* An Hsieh (A.D. 320 – A.D. 385): a general and statesman, and a renowned scholar in the Eastern Chin dynasty. An lived as a scholar-recluse until the country's crises required his service. Once North China fell to Chien Fu's invading troops. In A.D. 383, the barbarians advanced on the south, and Hsieh led an outnumbered Chin army that not only repelled the invasion but also disrupted the regime of Fore Ch'in, hence saving the Chinese race from being totally overrun.
* Ssuma: Hsiangju Ssuma (179 B.C.– 118 B.C.) in full name, a representative verse writer in Chinese literary history.
* Phoenix Array: the shining clothes Hsiangju Ssuma (179 B.C.– 118 B.C.) used to wear, made of a special kind of fur or hide.

赠宣城宇文太守兼呈崔侍御

白若白鹭鲜,
清如清唳蝉。
受气有本性,
不为外物迁。
饮水箕山上,
食雪首阳颠。
回车避朝歌,
掩口去盗泉。
岩峣广成子,
倜傥鲁仲连。
卓绝二公外,
丹心无间然。
昔攀六龙飞,
今作百炼铅。
怀恩欲报主,
投佩向北燕。
弯弓绿弦开,
满月不惮坚。
闲骑骏马猎,
一射两虎穿。
回旋若流光,
转背落双鸢。
胡房三叹息,
兼知五兵权。
枪枪突云将,
却掩我之妍。
多逢剿绝儿,

先著祖生鞭。
据鞍空矍铄，
壮志竟谁宣。
蹉跎复来归，
忧恨坐相煎。
无风难破浪，
失计长江边。
危苦惜颓光，
金波忽三圆。
时游敬亭上，
闲听松风眠。
或弄宛溪月，
虚舟信洄沿。
颜公二十万，
尽付酒家钱。
兴发每取之，
聊向醉中仙。
过此无一事，
静谈秋水篇。
君从九卿来，
水国有丰年。
鱼盐满市井，
布帛如云烟。
下马不作威，
冰壶照清川。
霜眉邑中叟，
皆美太守贤。
时时慰风俗，
往往出东田。
竹马数小儿，
拜迎白鹿前。

含笑问使君，
日晚可回旋？
遂归池上酌，
掩抑清风弦。
曾标横浮云，
下抚谢朓肩。
楼高碧海出，
树古青萝悬。
光禄紫霞杯，
伊昔忝相传。
良图扫沙漠，
别梦绕旌旃。
富贵日成疏，
愿言杳无缘。
登龙有直道，
倚玉阻芳筵。
敢献绕朝策，
思同郭泰船。
何言一水浅？
似隔九重天。
崔生何傲岸，
纵酒复谈玄。
身为名公子，
英才苦迍邅。
鸣凤托高梧，
凌风何翩翩。
安知慕群客，
弹剑拂秋莲。

To Yüwen, Magistrate of Hsuan While Presented to Royal Servant Ts'ui

White like a heron, pure as snow,
Clear like cicadas shrilling through.
What is nature in nature lies,
Not at all influenced otherwise.
Freedom at Dustpan drank a flow;
Ee and Ch'i at Firstshine ate snow.
Off Mornsong Sir Ink turned his cart;
From Thief Spring Sir Con kept apart.
For grace Harvest had a good name;
For charm Chunglien had a good fame.
These two men are beyond compare;
Who else can be so fair and square?
I used to seek favor before;
Now for elixir I cleanse ore.
And to requite our Lord's favor,
I once went to the cold border.
With much force I drew the green bow,
So full like the moon, like the glow.
When free, I whipped my horse to trot;
At one blow two tigers were shot.
I turned round like a flashing light,
And two hawks were killed while in flight.
With sighs the Huns did at me cower,
And I learned the strategist power.
The generals, so jealous of me,
Threw slanders, as vile as can be.

Most of them would put me to rout;
Cracking my whip, I ran about.
Now an old man, galloping still,
To whom could I express my will?
Time went away and then came back;
I sat with all worries, alack.
Without wind, I couldn't make way,
And to Prince E'er's camp I did stray.
I still cherished my aim, though old;
It had been three months, with waves gold.
Mt. Chingt'ing I did often climb
And lay amid pines to kill time.
I saw the Wan Stream greet the moon,
Letting my void boat float alone.
I was given much money, fine,
But I spent all of it on wine.
When I felt like drinking a cup,
In a wine shop I would cheer up.
Except this, nothing I would care,
Oft reading *Autumn Water* there.
From the headquarters you have come,
And there's a good gain, a good sum.
The market full of salt and fish,
And brocade for everyone's wish.
You are here, not swaggering on,
Like a jade kettle brightly shone.
The old folks aged with gray hair,
All praise you for your being square.
You oft come out and folks you calm,
And betimes inspect the East Farm.
A few kids riding high come near,

And bow down before your white deer.
I smile and ask you: Magistrate:
Will you go back now it's so late?
Why not have a cup by the pool
And play the lute in a breeze cool?
Like the floating cloud, you're so fair,
Even T'iao Hsieh could not compare.
The tower overlooks the blue sea;
The trailer creeps round the old tree.
You gave me a cloud cup before,
And I have cherished it, e'er more.
I've had the plan to fight the foe;
The flags in my dream in vain flow.
My dream for success is now nil;
A wish is so hard to fulfill.
To the court there rolls a broad way;
Slanderers always come to sway.
I've made bold to advise the court
And rowed with a hermit to sport.
Who says so shallow a brook is?
It may stop one like an abyss.
Ts'ui, so great, is oft in wine drowned,
And he'd discuss something profound.
Although he is a noble childe,
This talent's banished to the wild.
A phoenix perches on phoenix trees
Or soars up high against a breeze.
Who knows one who admires a crowd
With his sword sighs to lilies loud?

* Hsuan: a prefecture and a city in today's Anhui Province.

* heron: a long-necked and long-legged wading bird, a symbol of freedom, purity, longevity and happiness.
* cicada: a homopterous insect that sings its song of summer and shrills in autumn, a symbol of death and resurrection in Chinese culture because of its metamorphosis and recycle. Therefore, in ancient China, a jade cicada figure was put in the mouth of a dead body with such an intention of eternal life.
* Dustpan: a place in present-day Shantung Province. It's said that Mound visited Yu Hsu at Dustpan and intended to abdicate the throne to him. Hsu felt that he did not deserve it, however, and retreated to a farming life at Dustpan.
* Firstshine: Mt. Firstshine, located in today's Weiyüan County. It is the highest of all mountains there, so it is the first to receive sunshine, hence the name, and it is famous because two princes from the State of Lonebamboo called Bowone and Straightthree died of starvation here for their rectitude.
* Ee and Ch'i: referring to Bowone and Straightthree, childes in the late Shang dynasty. As they failed to admonish King Martial of Chough, they left King Chough and refused to take crops reaped under the reign of Chough. They lived on fungi on Mt. Firstshine and starved to death in the end.
* Mornsong: Chaoke if transliterated, the capital of Shang, in today's Ch'i County, Hopi, Honan Province.
* Sir Ink: Sir Ink (cir. 476 B.C.– 390 B.C.), a philosopher, educator, scientist, martial strategist in the late Spring and Autumn period and the early Warring States period, and the founder of Inkism which was regarded as one of the two most prestigious schools along with Confucianism. He came up with the Inkist ideas such as universal love, denouncing unjust war, and respecting scholars, which has exerted a great influence in Chinese history. Sir Ink turned his cart when he traveled nearby Mornsong, believing it a decadent place.
* Thief Spring: an ancient spring in today's Shantung Province. It's said that Confucius refused to drink the water from Thief Spring for the spring had an improper name.
* Harvest: referring to Sir Goodharvest, a legendary immortal who is said to have lived 1,200 years.
* Chunglien: Chunglien (B.C. 305 – 245 B.C.), referring to Chunglien Lu, a sophist from Ch'i in the late Spring and Autumn period. He declined to be titled and awarded by Lord Plain of Chao, and left for East Sea.
* Prince E'er: Prince E'er (? – A.D.757), the 16th son of Emperor Deepsire of T'ang. He was assigned to guard the south during Lushan An's Rebellion.
* Mt. Chingt'ing: an offset of Mt. Yellow, which is located nearby Hsuan. It consists of 60 peaks, rolling more than three miles and 317 meters above sea level, a mountain

with many literary legacies.
* *Autumn Water*: a fable in *Sir Lush*, an important book in the Spring and Autumn period.
* deer: a ruminant, the prototype of a unicorn in Chinese culture and a white deer being a Wordist symbol often seen in Chinese paintings: the mild animal ridden by an immortal.
* T'iao Hsieh: T'iao Hsieh (A.D. 464 – A.D. 499), an outstanding highborn landscape poet.
* Ts'ui: referring to Ts'ui, the royal servant.

赠宣城赵太守悦

赵得宝符盛,
山河功业存。
三千堂上客,
出入拥平原。
六国扬清风,
英声何喧喧?
大贤茂远业,
虎竹光南藩。
错落千丈松,
虬龙盘古根。
枝下无俗草,
所植唯兰荪。
忆在南阳时,
始承国士恩。
公为柱下史,
脱绣归田园。
伊昔簪白笔,
幽都逐游魂。
持斧冠三军,
霜清天北门。
差池宰两邑,
鹗立重飞翻。
焚香入兰台,
起草多芳言。
夔龙一顾重,
矫翼凌翔鹓。
赤县扬雷声,

强项闻至尊。
惊飙颓秀木，
迹屈道弥敦。
出牧历三郡，
所居猛兽奔。
迁人同卫鹤，
谬上懿公轩。
自笑东郭履，
侧惭狐白温。
闲吟步竹石，
精义忘朝昏。
憔悴成丑士，
风云何足论？
猕猴骑土牛，
羸马夹双辕。
愿借羲皇景，
为人照覆盆。
溟海不振荡，
何由纵鹏鲲。
所期玄津白，
倜傥假腾骞。

To Yüeh Chao, Magistrate of Hsuan

Chao became Crown Prince, charm in hand,
And his state prospered, town or land.
With his three thousand hangers-on,
He, much adored, was a strong one.
The Chao's gave Six States a fresh air;
Their great names rang, what a blare!

Your fathers' cause you carry on,
Now magistrate of the south town.
You offspring stand like erect pines;
From root to top creep aged vines.
Below the twigs grows grass rare,
Behold, orchids and iris there.
When I was in Southshine, a guest,
You saw me as a talent blessed.
As Censor, you did all alarm;
Your robe doffed, you went back to farm.
On my ear I once laid my white brush
And to chase north ghosts I did rush.
With my axe, the foes I did cow;
At North Gate I scared them enow.
You have been a magistrate twice,
Just like a fish hawk that twice flies.
Incense burned, I climbed Orchid Mound;
I wrote reports frank and profound.
Our Lord gave me much grace and love;
Like a hawk I flew high above.
My name like thunder shook the land;
Our Lord knew I could erect stand.
When a high wind strikes the best wood,
More obvious is my rectitude.
You have been a magistrate thrice,
And repelled evil shouts and cries.
Like Lord of Watch's crane, I would dart
And haply lighted on His cart.
I laughed I was in Easton's shoes,
And felt shame at white-furs like those.
I crooned and strolled the grove when free

And forgot how late it might be.
I felt myself haggard and slow;
How could I discuss come-and-go?
How can a monkey ride an ox?
How can a nag outrun a fox?
May I borrow light from the sun
To light up the bowl-covered one.
If the ocean no wind here brings
How can a roc spread out its wings?
One day may you climb up the mound!
By your wind I could fly, sky-bound.

* Chao: referring to Hsiangtzu Chao or Wuhsu Chao (? – 425 B.C.), a minister of Chin in the late Spring and Autumn period, and the founding lord of Chao in the Warring States period. Chao, though the second son, earned his title by memorizing the admonitions that his father wrote on bamboo slips.
* He, much adored, was a strong one: "he" refers to Lord Plain of Chao, one of the Four Childes in the Warring States Period who was generous and noble enough to attract many hangers-on in his house.
* incense: an aromatic substance that exhales perfume during combustion, offered to a Buddhist, Wordist or any religious or ancestral figure as an act of worship, usually during prayer.
* Orchid Mound: implying a censorate.
* Lord of Watch's crane: Lord Good of Watch (? – 660 B.C.), the eighteenth king of the State of Watch, was so fond of cranes that he even gave them carts, positions and salaries, incurring grievances from his officials. When Red Hunters invaded Watch, Lord Good rose up to launch a counter-attack, but some of his armymen turned traitor and his officials held him up to ridicule, replying:"Let the cranes fight."
* Easton: a man from Ch'i in the Western Han dynasty who was too poor to have a pair of good shoes. When he walked in snow, he was almost barefooted for the soles of his shoes were missing.
* white-furs: Ancient Chinese used white fox furs to make warm clothes. White-furs, thus, implies a life of luxury.
* monkey: any of a group of primates usually having a flat, hairless face, elongate

limbs, hands and feet adapted for grasping, and a highly developed nervous system, including marmosets, baboons, and macaques. They are not the anthropoid apes, though monkeys and apes are used alternatively in Chinese, also used as a metaphor for somebody who is mischievous and shrewdly calculating.
* ox: any of several bovid ruminants as cattle, buffaloes, bison, gaur, and yaks; especially a domesticated bull (Bos taurus), used as a draft animal, a symbol of diligence in Chinese culture.
* nag: a worn-out, old or inferior horse, a metaphor for a worthless person.
* fox: a burrowing canine mammal (genus *Vulpes*) having a long pointed muzzle and a long bushy tail, commonly reddish-brown in color, characterized by its cunning.

赠从弟宣州长史昭

淮南望江南，
千里碧山对。
我行倦过之，
半落青天外。
宗英佐雄郡，
水陆相控带。
长川豁中流，
千里泻吴会。
君心亦如此，
包纳无小大。
摇笔起风霜，
推诚结仁爱。
讼庭垂桃李，
宾馆罗轩盖。
何意苍梧云，
飘然忽相会？
才将圣不偶，
命与时俱背。
独立山海间，
空老圣明代。
知音不易得，
抚剑增感慨。
当结九万期，
中途莫先退。

To My Cousin, Glare, Secretary of Hsuan

From South Huai to South Land I gaze;
The green mountains each other face.
So tired, this place I now go by,
Half the mountains out of the sky.
As a great pillar of the crown,
You govern a water-land town.
The Yangtze rushes in the dale
A thousand miles south with a hail.
Your chest is like the Yangtze wide,
Which can contain all, wave and tide.
Good verse does rush out of your mind;
You are so sincere, frank and kind.
All disputes you can settle well;
Carts and steeds swarm in the hotel.
Like a cloud drifting here and there;
I've ne'er thought I could meet you e'er.
Gifted, I'm not used by the crown;
My destiny must have come down!
Alone between hills and the main;
In this heyday, I age in vain.
A real friend is hard to come by;
Stroking my sword, long, long I sigh.
Let's make a nine-millennia date;
Don't quit half way, early or late.

* South Huai: the area south of the Huai River.
* South Land: the area south of the Yangtze River.

* the Yangtze: the lower part of the Long River, that is, from Nanking to its estuary in Shanghai.
* stroking my sword: alluding to Pai Li's swordsmanship. When a bursting youth, Pai Li exhibited a swashbuckling penchant, took to knight-errantry, and learned swordmanship from Min P'ei, First Swordsman, a universally acknowledged swordsman in the T'ang dynasty, and as Pai Li boasted, second only to P'ei, he even slashed several combatants with his cutlass.

于五松山赠南陵常赞府

为草当作兰,
为木当作松。
兰秋香风远,
松寒不改容。
松兰相因依,
萧艾徒丰茸。
鸡与鸡并食,
鸾与鸾同枝。
拣珠去沙砾,
但有珠相随。
远客投名贤,
真堪写怀抱。
若惜方寸心,
待谁可倾倒?
虞卿弃赵相,
便与魏齐行。
海上五百人,
同日死田横。
当时不好贤,
岂传千古名。
愿君同心人,
于我少留情。
寂寂还寂寂,
出门迷所适。
长铗归来乎,
秋风思归客。

To Ch'ang, Magistrate of Southridge, at Mt. Five Pines

Be an orchid if grass you'd be;
See a cypress if wood you'd see.
An orchid sends afar its balm;
A cypress bears all cold or harm.
Cypress and orchid make a twain;
Wormwood and brushwood thrive in vain.
Chicken with chicken peck their food;
Phoenix with phoenix share their wood.
Pick up the pearl, throw out the sand,
And just keep the pearl in your hand.
A guest running to a man best
Can tell his woe and on him rest.
If in your chest you keep your thought,
To whom can you pour the whole lot?
Yü gave his premiership away,
And escaped side by side with Way.
The five hundred men on the sea
That day with Heng T'ien ceased to be.
If the best had not sought the same;
How could they for e'er pass their fame?
As in the same boat we would be,
Please pay some attention to me.
A lonesome bore, a lonesome bore,
I feel lost once out of the door.
Return, long sword, return, long sword.
In the wind I miss my home's ford.

* orchid: a terrestrial or epiphytic monocotyledonous plant, one of the four most important floral images in Chinese literature, which are wintersweet, orchid, bamboo, and chrysanthemum.
* cypress: an evergreen tree of the family Cupressaceae, having durable timber, a symbol of rectitude, nobility and longevity in Chinese culture.
* wormwood: any of a genus (*Artemisia*) of herbs or small shrubs related to the sagebrush, especially a common species, aromatic, tonic, bitter, and used in making absinthe.
* brushwood: a low thicket; underwood.
* Mt. Five Pines: located in today's T'ungling, Anhui Province, so named because there once grew five pines on the very top of the mountain. According to *Geographical Wonders* compiled in the Southern Sung dynasty, "The mountain boasted old pines, five in one, a pentad, reaching high to the sky with scale-like bark on the trunk."
* Yü: a minister of Chao in the Warring States period who insisted on making an alliance with Way and Ch'u to go against the strong Ch'in. When Ch'i Way came for help, Yü left the high position with Way, knowing his lord would not help.
* Way: referring to Ch'i Way, the prime minister of Way, who was a foe of Ch'in.
* Heng T'ien: Heng T'ien (? – 202 B.C.), a chief of an uprising at the end of Ch'in. T'ien refused to be reigned by Pang Liu and committed suicide at Firstshine. His five hundred followers drowned themselves when hearing the news.

自梁园至敬亭山见会公谈陵阳山水兼期同游因有此赠

我随秋风来,
瑶草恐衰歇。
中途寡名山,
安得弄云月?
渡江如昨日,
黄叶向人飞。
敬亭惬素尚,
弭棹流清辉。
冰谷明且秀,
陵峦抱江城。
粲粲吴与史,
衣冠耀天京。
水国饶英奇,
潜光卧幽草。
会公真名僧,
所在即为宝。
开堂振白拂,
高论横青云。
雪山扫粉壁,
墨客多新文。
为余话幽栖,
且述陵阳美。
天开白龙潭,
月映清秋水。
黄山望石柱,
突兀谁开张?

黄鹤久不来，
子安在苍茫。
东南焉可穷，
山鸟飞绝处。
稠叠千万峰，
相连入云去。
闻此期振策，
归来空闭关。
相思如明月，
可望不可攀。
何当移白足，
早晚凌苍山？
且寄一书札，
令予解愁颜。

Coming to See Mr. Hui at Mt. Chingt'ing, Talking About Hills and Rills of Ridgeshine and Hoping to Tour There Together, Hence the Poem

I come here with an autumn sough;
The magic herbs are withered now.
There're no famous hills on the way;
Where can I the moon and clouds play?
I got 'cross the river last night;
There greeted me a leaf in flight.
Mt. Chingt'ing can make virtues grow;
The boat sees the moon with waves glow.
The dale's bright, beautiful and chill;
The river town's hugged by the hill.

The guests gleam in robe or gown,
That can outshine Capital Town.
In this wetland talents abide,
Like orchids in rampant grass hide.
You are a real great monk, friend mine,
Where you are, you make the place shine.
White hossu swayed, you start to speak,
Like a stream gurgling down a peak.
With snow mountains drawn on the wall,
The scholars now write in the hall.
You ask me where I would abide,
And describe Ridgeshine's charming side.
White Dragon Abyss is divine,
Wherein the moon does coolly shine.
The Stone Pole on Mt. Yellow there
Thrusts up, a piece of art so rare.
It's long since Yellow Crane left here;
Where is the fairy now, o where?
Look southeast, is she there? Alas,
It's a place e'en birds cannot pass.
Hills upon hills make many crowds
That stretch out and rise to the clouds.
At such a place I feel o'erjoyed,
And I would practice there, all void.
But thinking is like the moon bright,
You can see it but can't there flight.
When will Whitefeet come here once more?
When can we o'er the mountains soar?
Do write me and do let me know
To relieve my frown and my woe.

- * Mt. Chingt'ing: a mountain with literary attractions, located nearby Hsuan in today's Anhui Province. It is an offset of Mt. Yellow, consisting of 60 peaks, rolling more than three miles and 317 meters above sea level, a mountain with many literary legacies.
- * orchid: a terrestrial or epiphytic monocotyledonous plant having thickened bulbous roots and often very showy distinctive flowers, one of the four most important floral images in Chinese literature, which are wintersweet, orchid, bamboo, and chrysanthemum.
- * white hossu: a white brush carried by the Wordist priest to dust or used as a weapon for defense, usually a symbol of purity and cleanliness.
- * Ridgeshine: referring to Lingyang if transliterated, a county located in present-day Anhui Province. According to legends, Sir Glare became immortal half way to Mt. Ridgeshine.
- * Mt. Yellow: located in today's Anhui Province. Mt. Yellow is one of the most famous mountains in China with natural, literary and cultural attractions, featured with wondrous pines, clouds and hotsprings. It is said that Lord Yellow used to make elixirs here.
- * the fairy: referring to Tzu-an, the immortal who is said to ride a yellow crane around.
- * Whitefeet: a monk in the T'ang dynasty.

赠友人三首
To My Friends, Three Poems

其 一

兰生不当户，
别是闲庭草。
夙被霜露欺，
红荣已先老。
谬接瑶华枝，
结根君王池。
顾无馨香美，
叨沐清风吹。
馀芳若可佩，
卒岁长相随。

No. 1

An orchid does not grow at door;
In a bare court, grass it would be.
It was bullied by frost before;
Now its early fade one can see.
Laid on a jade tree by mistake,
It roots there by Imperial Pool.
No more fragrance it can make,
Caressed in vain by an air cool.
If some perfume to it adheres,
It'd keep it for remaining years.

* orchid: any of a widely distributed family of terrestrial or epiphytic monocotyledonous plants having thickened bulbous roots and often very showy distinctive flowers, one of the four most important floral images in Chinese literature, which are wintersweet, orchid, bamboo, and chrysanthemum.
* Imperial Pool: referring to any pool in a palace.

其 二

袖中赵匕首，
买自徐夫人。
玉匣闭霜雪，
经燕复历秦。
其事竟不捷，
沦落归沙尘。
持此愿投赠，
与君同急难。
荆卿一去后，
壮士多摧残。
长号易水上，
为我扬波澜。
凿井当及泉，
张帆当济川。
廉夫唯重义，
骏马不劳鞭。
人生贵相知，
何必金与钱？

No. 2

Chao's dagger in the long sleeve hides,
Bought from Buck Hsu, a swordsmith great.
Brilliant, in the cask it abides,
Once passed to Ch'in from the Yan State.
As the plan was then unfulfilled,
It had been thrown to lie in dust.
Now I'll give it to you, well-willed;

It'll share your hardship you can trust.
When Chingk'e failed and died, no more,
Destroyed were many gallants brave.
You may hear someone cry ashore;
The Change throws to me a large wave.
To dig a well, water you'd see;
To set a sail, you'd reach the shore.
A righteous man should faithful be;
A fine horse needs no whip, no more.
In life true friendship is so rare;
For gold or cash we should not care.

* Buck Hsu: referring to Fujen Hsu, a swordsmith from Chao. The dagger that Chingk'e used to assassinate King of Ch'in was bought from him.
* Ch'in: the Ch'in State or the State of Ch'in (905 B.C.- 206 B.C.), enfeoffed as a dependency of Chough by King Piety of Chough in 905 B.C. and enfeoffed as a vassal state by King Peace of Chough in 770 B.C. In the ten years from 230 B.C. to 221 B.C., Ch'in wiped out the other six powers and became the first unified regime of China, i.e. the Ch'in Empire.
* Chingk'e: an assassin from Yan who attempted to kill Emperor First of Ch'in but failed.
* the Change: referring to the River Change, by which Chingk'e bade farewell to his lord and friend, and set off for his mission.

其 三

慢世薄功业，
非无胸中画。
谑浪万古贤，
以为儿童剧。
立产如广费，
匡君怀长策。
但苦山北寒，
谁知道南宅？
岁酒上逐风，
霜鬓两边白。
蜀主思孔明，
晋家望安石。
时人列五鼎，
谈笑期一掷。
虎伏被胡尘，
渔歌游海滨。
弊裘耻妻嫂，
长剑托交亲。
夫子秉家义，
群公难与邻。
莫持西江水，
空许东溟臣。
他日青云去，
黄金报主人。

No. 3

The world I spurn, ranks I ignore,

Not because I've no plan in store.
What is seen as saintly or sage
Is but children's farce on the stage.
Great expense I can well afford;
I've a great plan to aid the Lord.
Now the North Hill is harsh and cold;
Where is the South Mansion, behold?
Some wine please, drive the cold away;
My sideburns are tinged with frost, gray.
Great Glare the Shu Lord did look for;
Chin's Crown did Steady Stone adore.
With five tripods they did dine
And threw all gold while drinking wine.
Lurking Tiger did Hun dust don;
And ashore heard a song ring on.
Su's tatters did his dear ones fright;
Feng's sword his parents kept so tight.
To your family you're austere,
And your colleagues would not get near.
The West River rolls far away;
You can't the east man's thirst allay.
One day with clouds if I could stay,
With gold my host I would repay.

* the South Mansion: the mansion that Ch'üan Sun gave to Yü Chou.
* Great Glare: referring to Bright Chuke (A.D. 181 – A.D. 234), a statesman and strategist, the prime minister of the Kingdom of Shu in the Three Kingdoms period (A.D. 220 – A.D. 265).
* Steady Stone: the courtesy name of An Hsieh (A.D. 320 – A.D. 385), a statesman and renowned scholar in the Eastern Chin dynasty.
* tripod: a cooking utensil or cauldron with three feet or legs, usually cast with bronze, popular in ancient China, a symbol of a powerful family.

* Su: referring to Wu Su (140 B.C.- 60 B.C.), a minister of Han. On his diplomatic mission, Su was detained. The Huns tried to make him surrender with threats and promises, only to fail. Then, he was sent to North Sea, i.e., today's Baikal Lake, to be a shepherd. Through all kinds of hardship, Su finally came back to Han after 19 years' detention, during which time, Wu Su had never surrendered.
* Feng: referring to Yüan Feng, a strategist from Ch'i. When Feng was a hanger-on, he flipped his sword to ask for benefits since he had his parents to support. Seeing the generosity of his lord, he determined to serve him devotedly.

陈情赠友人

延陵有宝剑，
价重千黄金。
观风历上国，
暗许故人深。
归来挂坟松，
万古知其心。
懦夫感达节，
壮士激青衿。
鲍生荐夷吾，
一举置齐相。
斯人无良朋，
岂有青云望。
临财不苟取，
推分固辞让。
后世称其贤，
英风邈难尚。
论交但若此，
友道孰云丧。
多君骋逸藻，
掩映当时人。
舒文振颓波，
秉德冠彝伦。
卜居乃此地，
共井为比邻。
清琴弄云月，
美酒娱冬春。
薄德中见捐，

忽之如遗尘。
英豪未豹变,
自古多艰辛。
他人纵以疏,
君意宜独亲。
奈向成离居,
相去复几许。
飘风吹云霓,
蔽目不得语。
投珠冀相报,
按剑恐相距。
所思采芳兰,
欲赠隔荆渚。
沉忧心若醉,
积恨泪如雨。
愿假东壁辉,
馀光照贫女。

To My Friend, A Plaint

A precious sword Broadridge did hold;
'Twas worth a thousand taels of gold.
With his sword he traveled to Lu
And promised it in mind to Hsu.
He hung it o'er his tomb when back;
Then all knew he did not faith lack.
At this a coward feels debased,
And a gallant feels highly raised.
Shuya did Chung Kuan recommend
So that Chi could on him depend.

If Shuya had not had this friend,
How could they to the clouds ascend?
To properties he paid no heed,
And gave his own to those in need.
Descendants praised him as a sage,
Although he had come off the stage.
We should deal with people like this;
Who says the world has gone amiss?
Friend, you write so well, a best one;
All souls in the world you o'errun.
Your prose rushes o'er what's decayed;
Your worth obscures those finely made.
Drawing lots, the place you decide;
So we can now live side by side.
To the bright moon you pluck the string,
And your mellow wine lures the spring.
What is worthless you throw away;
What is debased you spurn as clay.
No tide comes for heroes to gain;
As always, heroes have much pain.
While others keep away from me,
You get near, a soul mate to be.
Now why do you from me depart?
And how long will we stay apart?
The ill wind darkens the sun bright;
Nothing we can say, blocked our sight.
Casting pearls, one expects a smile;
But someone keeps him off a mile.
I'd gather orchids for my soul,
But I am kept off by Bush Shoal.
I feel so sad as if I'll drown;

My wronged tears like a rain drip down.
I'd borrow some light from East Wall
So some luster on me may fall.

* Broadridge: a land of Wu in the Spring and Autumn period, belonging to Stripfour (576 B.C.- 484 B.C.), Chicha if transliterated, who declined the throne and farmed in Broadridge. Stripfour was an honest and righteous man. When Stripfour traveled to the State of Hsu, the lord of the state liked his sword but was reluctant to ask. Stripfour did not give the sword because his journey hadn't been finished. When Stripfour came back, he found the lord had already passed away, so he left his sword at the tomb to keep his words.
* Shuya and Chung Kuan: referring to Shuya Pao (? - 644 B.C.) and Chung Kuan (723 B.C.- 645 B.C.), statesmen and ministers of Ch'i, and true friends to each other.
* pearl: a smooth, lustrous, usually white and bluish-gray, calcareous concretion deposited in layers around a central nucleus in the shells of various mollusks or oysters, and largely used as a gem, medicine or given as a gift, a metaphor for the dearest one, a representation of nobility, purity and dignity in Chinese culture.
* orchid: a terrestrial or epiphytic monocotyledonous plants having thickened bulbous roots and often very showy distinctive flowers, one of the four most important floral images in Chinese literature, which are wintersweet, orchid, bamboo, and chrysanthemum.
* East Wall: There was a woman living in Ch'i who was so poor that had to borrow candle light from her neighbor when weaving cloth.

赠从弟冽

楚人不识凤,
重价求山鸡。
献主昔云是,
今来方觉迷。
自居漆园北,
久别咸阳西。
风飘落日去,
节变流莺啼。
桃李寒未开,
幽关岂来蹊。
逢君发花萼,
若与青云齐。
及此桑叶绿,
春蚕起中闺。
日出布谷鸣,
田家拥锄犁。
顾余乏尺土,
东作谁相携。
傅说降霖雨,
公输造云梯。
羌戎事未息,
君子悲涂泥。
报国有长策,
成功羞执珪。
无由谒明主,
杖策还蓬藜。
他年尔相访,

知我在磻溪。

To Li Li, My Cousin

Unable to phoenixes descry,
The Ch'u man a pheasant did buy.
I'd present my verse to the Lord;
I felt puzzled it was ignored.
Like Sir Lush lived in Lacquer Grove,
Far from the capital I rove.
A wind blows to the setting sun,
Orioles cry, the season gone.
Not yet in bloom are the peach trees;
How can the dale enjoy a breeze?
When you come, the blooms burst aloud,
Like brocade shining to the cloud.
The mulberries green begin to sprout;
The silkworms hatched now creep about.
The sun is up and cuckoos cry;
The farmers their plough afield ply.
I do not have a piece of land;
Who can lend me a helping hand?
Yüeh Fu caused rain to farmers aid,
And Pan Lu a cloud ladder made.
Against the barbarians the war
Goes on, and the pains I deplore.
I have good blueprints for the state;
I feel shy to hold a post great.
To see our Lord I have no way
And retreat to my shack to stay.

> If you come one day for a look,
> You know I fish by the Pan Brook.

* Sir Lush: Sir Lush (369 B.C.- 286 B.C.), a great thinker, philosopher and litterateur in the Warring States Period. As a principal founder of Wordism, Sir Lush enjoys as high a reputation as Laocius.
* Lacquer Grove: where Sir Lush worked when he was an official. A lacquer tree, from which resinous varnish can be extracted, is common in China and Japan.
* mulberry: the edible, berry-like juicy fruit of a tree (genus *Morus*) whose leaves are valued for silkworm culture, and the tree itself.
* silkworm: the larva of a moth that produces a dense silken cocoon, especially the common silkworm from whose cocoon commercial silk is made. The silkworm was cultivated in 3000 B.C. when Lace Mum, who was Lord Yellow's concubine began to raise silkworms and made silk.
* cuckoo: any of a family of birds with a long, slender body, grayish-brown on top and white below, a symbol of sadness in Chinese culture. As is said, during the Shang dynasty, Cuckoo (Yü Tu), a caring king of Shu, abdicated the throne due to a flood and lived in reclusion. After his death, he turned into a cuckoo, wailing day and night, shedding tears and blood.
* Yüeh Fu: Master Joy if transliterated, a noble minister of high reputation in the Shang dynasty. Historic records say that the King of Shang dreamed of a sage, and he sent people out to search for him and found Yüeh Fu.
* Pan Lu: Pan Lu (507 B.C.- 444 B.C.), an inventor, Father of Carpentry, from Lu in the Spring and Autumn period.
* the Pan Brook: where Great Grand went fishing. Great Grand was an influential strategist and statesman and a founder of Chough. Though he was a butcher at his young age, Great Grand remained diligent in hardship, expecting to display his ability for the country one day, but he did not make any achievement before he was 70 years old. He went west at the age of 72, fishing as he waited for King Civil, and finally won his appreciation.

赠闾丘处士

贤人有素业，
乃在沙塘陂。
竹影扫秋月，
荷衣落古池。
闲读山海经，
散帙卧遥帷。
且耽田家乐，
遂旷林中期。
野酌劝芳酒，
园蔬烹露葵。
如能树桃李，
为我结茅茨。

To Staff Knoll Lü

In fathers' estate you abide,
As is called Sand Pond Waterside.
The bamboo sweeps Luna with shade;
The lotus in the pool, decayed.
When idle, you read *Mounts and Seas*
While lying in your tent, at ease.
On the farm you have fun, elate;
Forgotten is your hermit's date.
In the field we have mellow wine;
On greens and sunflower seeds we dine.
More peaches and plums there can be,

And a few thatched shacks built for me.

* bamboo: a tall, tree-like or shrubby grass in tropical and semi-tropical regions, a symbol of integrity and altitude, one of the four most important images in Chinese literature, which are wintersweet, orchid, bamboo, and chrysanthemum.
* lotus: one of the various plants of the waterlily family, noted for their large floating round leaves and showy flowers blooming in white or pink, a symbol of purity and elegance in Chinese culture, unsoiled though out of soil, so clean with all leaves green.
* *Mounts and Seas*: a geographical book containing abundant tales, fables, mysterious creatures, folklore and rough understandings of medicines and races in the remote ages.
* plums and peaches: a metonymy for plants in general; a metaphor for disciples or students, and sometimes symbolizing a flashy life.

赠钱征君少阳

白玉一杯酒，
绿杨三月时。
春风馀几日，
两鬓各成丝。
秉烛唯须饮，
投竿也未迟。
如逢渭水猎，
犹可帝王师。

To Firstshine Ch'ien, a Recruit Not Accepting the Post

A white jade cup of mellow wine,
The willows sweeping the spring fine.
A few more days can spring wind blow;
Our sideburns begin to gray grow.
In candlelight we should now drink
Or angle by the fountain brink.
If the Lord hunts game by the Wei,
I'd be His Teacher the same day.

---

* willow: any of a large genus of shrubs and trees related to the poplars, having generally smooth branches, and often long, slender, pliant, and sometimes pendent branchlets, a symbol of farewell or nostalgia in Chinese culture. The best image of a weeping willow in Chinese literature is in *Vetch We Pick*, a verse in *The Book of Songs*, which is like this: When we left long ago, / The willows waved adieu. / Now back to our home town, / We meet snow falling down.

* the Wei: the Wei River: the largest branch of the Yellow River, originating from today's Mt. Birdmouse in Kansu Province, flowing through Precious Rooster, Allshine, Long Peace, and meeting the Yellow River at T'ung Pass.
* His Teacher: referring to Great Grand, an influential strategist and statesman in the Shang and Chough dynasties, the first marquis of Ch'i.

赠宣州灵源寺仲浚公

敬亭白云气，
秀色连苍梧。
下映双溪水，
如天落镜湖。
此中积龙象，
独许浚公殊。
风韵逸江左，
文章动海隅。
观心同水月，
解领得明珠。
今日逢支遁，
高谈出有无。

To Master Chün Chung at Soul Source Temple in Hsuan

Mt. Ching'ting sees all white clouds free
Rolling to Mt. Parasol Tree.
With their shadows in the Twin Streams,
The sky's in Mirror Lake it seems.
Here are hermits and talents blessed;
Out of them all you are the best.
Your flair and style strike one with awe;
Your prose and verse shake the seashore.
Your heart's like the watery moon;
You have got the Word all too soon.

> I seem to have met Master Flee,
> Now we could talk: be or not be.

* Mt. Chingt'ing: a mountain with literary attractions, located nearby Hsuan. It is an offset of Mt. Yellow, consisting of 60 peaks, rolling more than three miles and 317 meters above sea level, a mountain with many literary legacies.
* Mt. Parasol Tree: Mt. Nine Doubts, located in the south of today's Hunan Province.
* Mirror Lake: a large reservoir built in the Han dynasty, higher than the fields and the fields higher than the sea, 310 li in circumference.
* the Word: referring to Tao if transliterated, the most significant and profoundest concept in Chinese philosophy, comparable to God, the Word or the Logos in Western culture. The Word is fully elucidated in *The Word and the World*, the single book that Laocius wrote all his wisdom into. Its importance can be seen in this verse: "The Word is void, but its use is infinite. O deep! It seems to be the root of all things."
* Master Flee: a renowned monk in the Chin dynasty.

赠僧朝美

水客凌洪波,
长鲸涌溟海。
百川随龙舟,
嘘吸竟安在。
中有不死者,
探得明月珠。
高价倾宇宙,
馀辉照江湖。
苞卷金缕褐,
萧然若空无。
谁人识此宝,
窃笑有狂夫。
了心何言说,
各勉黄金躯。

To Mei Ch'ao, the Monk

The boatman on the waves does float
And nearby jumps out a long whale.
The tides and waves chase the boat,
Which sinks as the whale does inhale.
There survives one—he does not die;
And instead he gains a pearl bright.
Its price soars up to the blue sky
While to lakes and seas it sheds light.
It can surpass the clothes of gold;

All gems fade away to be none.
This treasure great who can behold?
Who braves you or me, a mad one?
We do not need to say so much;
Do take care of ourselves as such.

* whale: a cetaceous mammal of fish-like form, especially one of the larger pelagic species, as distinguished from dolphins and porpoises. Whales have the fore limbs developed as broad flattened paddles, hind limbs absent, and a thick layer of fat or blubber immediately beneath the skin. A whale is a symbol of great ambition, fortitude and uniqueness.
* pearl: a lustrous, calcareous concretion deposited in layers around a central nucleus in the shells of various mollusks, and largely used as a gem.

赠僧行融

梁有汤惠休，
常从鲍照游。
峨眉史怀一，
独映陈公出。
卓绝二道人，
结交凤与麟。
行融亦俊发，
吾知有英骨。
海若不隐珠，
骊龙吐明月。
大海乘虚舟，
随波任安流。
赋诗旃檀阁，
纵酒鹦鹉洲。
待我适东越，
相携上白楼。

To Jung Hsing, the Monk

In Liang, Hsiu by name, there was one
Who toured with Pao, going or gone.
On Mt. Brow, Embracing One there
With Tzu-ang Ch'en did brightly glare.
These two monks naturally born
Stayed with Phoenix or Unicorn.
You, a great master, as I know,

Just like them so brilliantly glow.
The deep sea can't eclipse the pearl;
Black Dragon does its brightness swirl.
The great sea carries the void boat,
Which follows the blue waves to float.
You write verse in Sandal Wood, glad;
You drink wine on Parrot Shoal, mad.
When I go see you in East Land,
Let's climb up White Tower hand in hand.

* Hsiu: referring to Huihsiu T'ang, a monk and poet who was asked to resume a secular life as an official because the Lord of Liang appreciated his poems.
* Pao: referring to Chao Pao (A.D. 414 – A.D. 466), a litterateur and poet from Sung (A.D. 420 – A.D. 479), the first kingdom of the Sixteen Dynasties.
* Mt. Brow: one of the four Buddhist mountains, located in Ssuch'uan Province, named for its elegant brow-shaped silhouette viewed from a distance.
* Embracing One: a renowned monk who liked making friends like Tzu-ang Ch'en.
* Tzu-ang Ch'en: Tzu-ang Ch'en (A.D. 661 – A.D. 702), a litterateur and poet in the T'ang dynasty.
* Phoenix: a certain phoenix. The phoenix is a legendary bird, king of all birds, a symbol of good luck and nobility.
* Unicorn: a certain unicorn. The unicorn is a divine deer-like animal with one horn, a symbol of saintliness in Chinese culture.
* Black Dragon: a black dragon mentioned in *Sir Lush*: "The dragon must have been asleep. If the dragon had woken up, could you have come back alive?" The black dragon is a gruesome monster though normally a dragon is a symbol of benevolence and sovereignty in Chinese culture.
* Parrot Shoal: a shoal located in Wuhan, Hupei Province. It is named for *Ode to the Parrot* by Heng Mi (A.D. 173 – A.D. 198), an upright man in the Three Kingdoms period. When Mi was banished to Wuhan, the magistrate gave him a parrot and required him to write a verse about it, hence *Ode to the Parrot*, comparing the parrot to himself.

赠黄山胡公求白鹇

　　闻黄山胡公有双白鹇，盖是家鸡所伏，自小驯狎，了无惊猜，以其名呼之，皆就掌取食。然此鸟耿介，尤难畜之，余平生酷好，竟莫能致。而胡公辍赠于我，唯求一诗。闻之欣然，适会宿意，援笔三叫，文不加点以赠之。

请以双白璧，
买君双白鹇。
白鹇白如锦，
白雪耻容颜。
照影玉潭里，
刷毛琪树间。
夜栖寒月静，
朝步落花闲。
我愿得此鸟，
玩之坐碧山。
胡公能辍赠，
笼寄野人还。

To Mr. Hu at Mt. Yellow, Who Gives Me Silver Pheasants as a Gift

　　I hear Mr. Hu at Mt. Yellow has a pair of silver pheasants. They were hatched by a hen and tamed while young with no frights or doubts at all. They, called as they are, have food from the keeper's palm. But they are stubborn, hard to keep. Though I am fond of birds, I cannot get near them. Mr. Hu takes them out and gives them to me as a gift, only asking for a poem. I feel happy about it and just feel like writing something. I pick up my writing brush, utter three shouts and finish the verse in one breath, hence the poem.

> I'll buy the silver pheasants bright
> For this pair of jadeite discs white.
> Silver pheasants like white brocade,
> Their white color makes blossoms fade.
> They by the moonlit abyss roam
> And amid flowers their feathers comb.
> At night, they perch on the calm tree;
> At dawn they stroll the blooms so free.
> I would have them and have their trills
> And play with them against the hills.
> If you, sir, could give them to me;
> In the wild mountains we will be.

* Mt. Yellow: located in today's Anhui Province. Mt. Yellow is one of the most famous mountains in China with natural, literary and cultural attractions, featured with wondrous pines, clouds and hotsprings. It's said that Lord Yellow used to make elixirs here, hence the name Yellow.
* pheasant: a long-tailed gallinaceous bird noted for the gorgeous plumage of the male.
* writing brush: any of various writing brushes or called Chinese brush, widely used for writing or painting, invented or renovated by Tien Meng (259 B.C.- 210 B.C.), a general in the Ch'in dynasty. It is one of the four treasures in a Chinese study, the other three stationeries being ink, paper and inkslab.

登敬亭山南望怀古赠窦主簿

敬亭一回首，
目尽天南端。
仙者五六人，
常闻此游盘。
溪流琴高水，
石耸麻姑坛。
白龙降陵阳，
黄鹤呼子安。
羽化骑日月，
云行翼鸳鸾。
下视宇宙间，
四溟皆波澜。
汰绝目下事，
从之复何难？
百岁落半途，
前期浩漫漫。
强食不成味，
清晨起长叹。
愿随子明去，
炼火烧金丹。

To Secretary T'ou When, Having Climbed Up Mt. Chingt'ing, I Gaze South While Thinking of the Past

On Mt. Chingt'ing I cast my eyes

Back to the south end of the skies.
Five or six fairies, I oft hear,
Stroll and seek pleasure around here.
The creek with a flute tune flows by;
Hemp Maid Altar mid peaks stands high.
The white dragon falls on the hill;
To Sir Peace the yellow cranes trill.
Riding a crane, Sir Peace soars high
With a phoenix up to the sky.
From the cosmos they look below;
The four oceans with their waves flow.
The worldly matters they despise,
Tho everything's hard neath the skies.
In life's century, I'm half way,
And can't predict the coming day.
What's grabbed to eat has no taste good;
At dawn I rise and sigh in mood.
I'd follow the hermit, Sir Glare
To refine cinnabar o'er there.

* Mt. Chingt'ing: a mountain with literary attractions, which is an offset of Mt. Yellow, located nearby Hsuan.
* Hemp Maid: an alternative name of Maid Flax, a mythical figure, who looks eighteen years old but claims to witness three times' drying-outs of the East Sea.
* The white dragon falls on the hill: Sir Glare, fond of fishing, once caught a white dragon. He felt scared and released it. Later, Glare got a white fish with a prescription in its body. He found all the ingredients and took them as elixir. Three years later, the white dragon came to pick him up onto a hill.
* Sir Peace: an immortal, who is said to ride a yellow crane around.
* phoenix: In Chinese myths, phoenixes, auspicious birds, unlike ordinary ones, only perch on parasol trees, and only eat bamboo shoots and pearly stone.
* cosmos: the world or universe considered as a system, perfect in order and arrangement, opposed to chaos.

* Sir Glare: an immortal from Riveroil in today's Ssuch'uan, who is said to have risen riding a white crane.
* cinnabar: a crystallized red mercuric sulfide, HgS, the chief ore of mercury, the raw mineral material for elixir in Wordist alchemy.

经乱后将避地剡中留赠崔宣城

双鹅飞洛阳，
五马渡江徼。
何意上东门，
胡雏更长啸。
太白昼经天，
颓阳掩馀照。
王城皆荡覆，
世路成奔峭。
四海望长安，
颦眉寡西笑。
苍生疑落叶，
白骨空相吊。
连兵似雪山，
破敌谁能料？
我垂北溟翼，
且学南山豹。
崔子贤主人，
欢娱每相召。
胡床紫玉笛，
却坐青云叫。
杨花满州城，
置酒同临眺。
忽思剡溪去，
水石远清妙。
雪尽天地明，
风开湖山貌。
闷为洛生咏，

醉发吴越调。
赤霞动金光,
日足森海峤。
独散万古意,
闲垂一溪钓。
猿近天上啼,
人移月边棹。
无以墨绶苦,
来求丹砂要。
华发长折腰,
将贻陶公诮。

To Ts'ui, Magistrate of Hsuan When I Seek Shelter in Mid-Shan at the Time of Unrest

Two geese fly from Loshine to stray;
Five steeds wade the river to neigh.
Over East Gate Hun hawks fly higher,
And shriek to the flaming war fire.
Venus shines much during the day;
The sun eclipsed leaves there a ray.
The capital town is erased;
The road is bumpy, lying waste.
Looking back to Long Peace for miles,
They shrink with sad tears, no more smiles.
The masses move like fallen leaves;
The white of bones to the bones grieves.
The troops are like the snow mountains;
Can they defeat Huns and chieftains?
I would spread wings over North Sea;

A leopard lurking I'd learn to be.
Magistrate Ts'ui, you're a good host;
You do ask me to feast or toast.
On the stool the mauve flute you play,
To lure clouds from the Milky Way.
Poplar catkins all o'er the town,
We drink and see them floating down.
Sudd'nly I'd go to the Shan Stream;
The flow o'er pebbles makes a dream.
The land's lightened by the new snow;
A wind o'er rills and hills does flow.
In mood like Lo, I learn to croon;
When drunk, I sing a southern tune.
The red clouds float on with light gold;
The sun sinks behind mountains cold.
I would dispel my age-long woe,
While the brook where I fish does flow.
Monkeys shriek, as if from the sky;
People to the moon their oars ply.
Don't be tired with ribbon and seal,
Making elixir can appeal.
If in prime you bow down like that,
By Ch'ien T'ao you will be laughed at.

* Two geese fly from Loshine: As is said, in the year of A.D. 305, a land in Loshine sank and two geese flied out, one black and the other white, as was considered by Wordists as an ill omen. Not long after, the Huns dragged the mainland into chaos.
* five steeds: In the Chin dynasty, there was a children's folklore, singing "Five steeds cross a river, and turn dragons together." Years later, when the mainland was in chaos, only five vassal clans survived.
* Hun hawks: indicating the army of Shih Le (A.D. 274 - A.D. 333), a Hun who occupied the northern lands. When Shih was 14, he traveled to Loshine with a group of

merchants. Shih leaned against East Gate and howled. Yan Wang (A.D. 256 – A.D. 311), a minister of West Chin, saw him and asserted that the boy would bring a calamity in future.

* Venus: In Chinese astrology, there will be a disaster when Venus shows up across the sky in the daytime.
* Long Peace: referring to Ch'ang'an if transliterated, the metropolis of gold, the capital of the T'ang Empire.
* wings over North Sea: According to *Sir Lush*, there is a minnow in North Sea. When it turns into a roc, its wings spread like clouds overwhelm the sky. The poet compares himself to the roc to demonstrate a strong desire of displaying his abilities.
* A leopard lurking: A leopard is a ferocious carnivorous mammal of the cat family. As legend goes, there is a black leopard on the South Hill. In foggy and rainy days, it will not eat for 7 days to keep its furs glossy, indicating a quality of staying away from trouble.
* stool: formerly called Hun stool, an armless and backless collapsible seat intended for one person, introduced to China in the Han dynasty.
* the Milky Way: the Silver River in Chinese mythology, a luminous band circling the heavens composed of stars and nebulae; the Galaxy.
* poplar: any of a genus (*Populus*) of dioecious trees and bushes of the willow family, widely distributed in the northern hemisphere.
* catkin: a deciduous scaly spike of flowers, as in the willow, an image of helpless drifting or wandering in Chinese literature.
* the Shan Stream: a main stream with rich cultural attractions in present-day Shengchow, Chechiang Province.
* Ch'ien T'ao: Poolbright T'ao or Yüanming T'ao (A.D. 352 – A.D. 427) if transliterated, a verse writer, poet, and litterateur in the Chin dynasty, and the founder of Chinese idyllism, who was once the magistrate of P'engtse.

献从叔当涂宰阳冰

金镜霾六国，
亡新乱天经。
焉知高光起，
自有羽翼生？
萧曹安屹屼，
耿贾摧欃枪。
吾家有季父，
杰出圣代英。
虽无三台位，
不借四豪名。
激昂风云气，
终协龙虎精。
弱冠燕赵来，
贤彦多逢迎。
鲁连善谈笑，
季布折公卿。
遥知礼数绝，
常恐不合并。
惕想结宵梦，
素心久已冥。
顾惭青云器，
谬奉玉樽倾。
山阳五百年，
绿竹忽再荣。
高歌振林木，
大笑喧雷霆。
落笔洒篆文，

崩云使人惊。
吐辞又炳焕,
五色罗华星。
秀句满江国,
高才掞天庭。
宰邑艰难时,
浮云空古城。
居人若薙草,
扫地无纤茎。
惠泽及飞走,
农夫尽归耕。
广汉水万里,
长流玉琴声。
雅颂播吴越,
还如泰阶平。
小子别金陵,
来时白下亭。
群凤怜客鸟,
差池相哀鸣。
各拔五色毛,
意重泰山轻。
赠微所费广,
斗水浇长鲸。
弹剑歌苦寒,
严风起前楹。
月衔天门晓,
霜落牛渚清。
长叹即归路,
临川空屏营。

To Sun Ice Li, My Uncle, Magistrate of Tangt'u

The great Way dims all o'er the land;
It's 'gainst Heaven to fall or stand.
Didn't High and Light mount the throne
Because their feathers had well grown?
Hsiao and Ts'ao stabilized the land;
Keng and Ch'ia destroyed a bad band.
You're like Uncle Youngest before,
A great, great hero evermore.
Tho you don't have a premier's place,
Nor depend on Four Gallants ace,
You with your high spirits do soar
And like a tiger with might roar.
You came from North at twenty then,
Greeted by many brilliant men.
Like Lien Lu, you oft smile and gin;
Like Pu Chi, all grandees you win.
Many men don't know rites I hear;
I can't deal well with them I fear.
In my dream, oft stricken with care,
I feel hurt and stroll in despair.
I have drunk so much of your wine;
I feel shy with you, a horse fine.
Five hundred years now from Hill Shine,
The bamboo thrives again, so fine.
Your loud song the forest does quake;
Your high laugh a thunder does shake.

You run your brush, a handsome seal;
The clouds and sky crack you may feel.
Your fluent words speak your brilliance,
Like five-hued stars give off radiance.
Your verse to this land is well known,
And your flair is praised by the throne.
You come here when the state comes down,
All hanging clouds o'er the void town.
The residents like cut-off grass,
Swept off, so few are left, alas.
Now the whole land enjoys your balm,
And people have come back to farm.
The Yangtze thousands of miles long
Flows on with your lute tune and song.
Psalms and odes ring over South Land
And to the sky above expand.
As away from Gold Hill I would go;
At White Bower all waved me adieu.
Phoenixes showed mercy on me
And released a loud whining plea.
Each gave me a pittance of plume;
A dwarfed air Mt. Arch did assume.
Despite the relief I spent too much,
Like a splash on a whale as such.
Swaying my sword, I sing a trill,
Like a sough starting from the sill.
To Heaven's Gate the moon does veer;
Frost coming down, Ox Shoal turns clear.
Let me go home, let me go back;
At the Yangtze I wonder, alack.

* Sun Ice Li: Yangping Li if transliterated, Pai Li's kinsman if not assumed, and a calligrapher of note. He, when Magistrate of Tangt'u, saved Pai Li from total ignominy in his last years and brought out his works in 762, the year of the latter's death. At the close of Pai Li's life Sun Ice nursed him through his failing health as a patron who was best equipped to understand him in his earthly weakness and crowning glory.
* High and Light: referring to Pang Liu (256 B.C.- 195 B.C.), Highsire of Han, the founding lord of West Han, and Hsiu Liu (6 B.C.- A.D. 57), Emperor Lightmight of Han, who re-established the governance of Han and started the reign of Eastern Han.
* Hsiao: referring to Ho Hsiao (257 B.C.- 193 B.C.), a statesman, the first prime minister and one of the Three Standouts in the early Han dynasty.
* Ts'ao: referring to Ts'an Ts'ao (? - 190 B.C.), the second prime minister of Han taking over from Ho Hsiao.
* Keng: referring to Yan Keng (A.D. 3 - A.D. 58), one of the founding commanders of Eastern Han.
* Ch'ia: referring to Fu Chia (A.D. 9 - A.D. 55), one of the founding commanders of Eastern Han.
* Uncle Youngest: referring to Liang Hsiang (? - 208 B.C.), a strategist in the late Ch'in and the uncle of Yü Hsiang (232 B.C.- 202 B.C.). He contributed a lot in the revolt against Ch'in.
* Four Gallants: referring to the four outstanding childes in the Warring States period, known as Lord Mengch'ang of Ch'i, Lord Plain of Chao, Lord Faithridge of Way and Lord Chunshen of Ch'u.
* Lien Lu: referring to Chunglien Lu (305 B.C.- 245 B.C.), a sophist from Ch'i in the late Spring and Autumn period. He declined to be titled and awarded by Lord Plain of Chao, and left for East Sea.
* Pu Chi: once a commander of Ch'u who defeated the Han's army several times. After Han won, Pu Chi hid himself and lived as a farm labourer for Chu. With the help of Chu, Pu Chi was pardoned by Pang Liu and became an imperial guard.
* Hill Shine: the place where Seven Sages of Bamboo Groves gathered, located in present-day Hue (Hui) County, Honan Province; a metonymy for that time, from A.D. 240 to A.D. 249.
* a handsome seal: suggesting the calligrapher Sun Ice is good at seal, a style of handwriting, often used on seals, widely used before the Han Dynasty.
* Gold Hill: present-day Nanking, one of the most well-known ancient capital cities in China.
* White Bower: a post not far from East Gate of Gold Hill, that is, today's Nanking.

* phoenix: In Chinese myths, phoenixes, auspicious birds, unlike ordinary ones, only perch on parasol trees, and only eat bamboo shoots and pearly stone.
* Mt. Arch: the first of the Five Sacred Mountains in China, located in Shantung Province, along with Mt. Ever in Shanhsi, Mt. Scale in Hunan, Mt. Flora in Sha'anhsi, and Mt. Tower in Honan.
* Heaven's Gate: a name shared by many mountains. The one here may indicate a mountain that immortals dwell.
* Ox Shoal: an ancient town in present-day Anhui Province.
* The Yangtze: the Yangtze River or the lower reaches of the Long River.

书怀赠南陵常赞府

岁星入汉年,
方朔见明主。
调笑当时人,
中天谢云雨。
一去麒麟阁,
遂将朝市乖。
故交不过门,
秋草日上阶。
当时何特达,
独与我心谐。
置酒凌歔台,
欢娱未曾歇。
歌动白纻山,
舞回天门月。
问我心中事,
为君前致辞。
君看我才能,
何似鲁仲尼。
大圣犹不遇,
小儒安足悲。
云南五月中,
频丧渡泸师。
毒草杀汉马,
张兵夺云旗。
至今西洱河,
流血拥僵尸。
将无七擒略,

鲁女惜园葵。
咸阳天下枢,
累岁人不足。
虽有数斗玉,
不如一盘粟。
赖得契宰衡,
持钧慰风俗。
自顾无所用,
辞家方来归。
霜惊壮士发,
泪满逐臣衣。
以此不安席,
蹉跎身世违。
终当灭卫谤,
不受鲁人讥。

To Ts'ang, Magistrate of Southridge

That year Jupiter fell to Han;
The divine Lord had a wise man.
My colleagues I used to deride,
And for this I was laid aside.
From Letters Hall I did depart;
And for long I wandered apart.
My friends no longer made a call,
Wild grass overgrown on the wall.
Howe'er, you're especially kind;
Harmonious with me, mind to mind.
Atop Rising Mound you place wine;
Our pleasure tends not to decline.

Over Mt. White Hemp rings a croon;
Heaven Gate dances charm the moon.
You ask me why I feel depressed;
Let me to you make a clean breast.
Do you think my talent is true?
Can I outshine Confucius in Lu?
E'en he was not used by the Lord;
How should I have myself deplored?
O'er there in Yünnan, the fifth moon,
The Lord's troops fell down all too soon.
Their steeds were in weeds trodden down;
Their banners were so rapped and torn.
The West Ear River flows with blood
O'er corpses. What a stinky flood!
The marshal has no skills to ply;
The folks like Lu's girls to blooms sigh.
Allshine's the hub of the world so great,
But the folks have no food to eat.
One may have big crates of jade nice,
But it can't match a plate of rice.
Blessed with someone like Ch'i of yore,
We've good manners, and hope in store.
Of no use, caliber I lack;
I wander out, not yet gone back.
To his gray hair a warrior sighs;
The exile's gown soaked with tears dries.
At night, sleepless, I toss and turn;
In this hard time, my heart does burn.
I'll dispel all slanders some day,
Not judged and sneered at anyway.

* Jupiter: the fifth planet from the sun, around which it revolves about 12 years at a mean distance of 483,000,000 miles. And Jupiter is a year in Chinese astronomy because its orbit, close to the ecliptic, is divided into twelve parts, which represent 12 years, and accordingly one year is called one Jupiter year, Jupiter for short.
* Letters Hall: a palace of the Han dynasty, implying the court.
* Rising Mound: a mound on Mt. Yellow, a summer resort built by Emperor Martial of Sung (A.D. 363 – A.D. 422).
* Mt. White Hemp: 2.5 kilometers from Tangt'u County, originally called Mt. Ch'u.
* Heaven Gate: referring to Mt. Heaven Gate or Mt. Sky Gate.
* Confucius: Confucius (551 B.C.- 479 B.C.), a renowned thinker, educator and statesman in the Spring and Autumn period, born in the State of Lu, who was the founder of Confucianism and who has exerted profound influence on Chinese culture.
* a wise man: referring to Newmoon East (Shuo Tungfang) (154 B.C.- 93 B.C.), a jocular and witted official serving Lord Martial of Han. The poet compares himself to Newmoon East.
* the West Ear River: referring to Ear Sea in today's Yünan Province. T'ang army had a fierce fight in Yünan.
* Lu's girl: There was a girl in Lu, unmarried when in her marriageable age. She sighed in her garden, and her neighbor thought she was sighing for not being engaged. The girl explained that she was sighing for the lord was getting old but the prince was too little to stabilize the country, which would trigger a chaos when the old lord passed away.
* Ch'i: a meritorious minister who helped Worm with a water project in remote history.

赠 汪 伦

李白乘舟将欲行，
忽闻岸上踏歌声。
桃花潭水深千尺，
不及汪伦送我情。

To Lun Wang

While I'm leaving now to the boat embark,
A song from the bank treads in with beats, hark.
A thousand feet deep is the Peach Bloom Pond,
But not deeper than my friend's love so fond.

* the Peach Bloom Pond: a pond in Ching County under the jurisdiction of Hsuan, with a bucolic scene of Peach Blossom Source depicted by Lord Glee, that is, Lingyün Hsieh (A.D. 385 - A.D. 433). Here, a villager called Lun Wang treated Pai Li with wine and saw him off with the simplicity of true love. Lun's descendants cherish this poem till now.

古近体诗二十五首
Old-new Rhythmic Poetry, 25 Poems

安陆白兆山桃花岩寄刘侍御绾

云卧三十年,
好闲复爱仙。
蓬壶虽冥绝,
鸾鹤心悠然。
归来桃花岩,
得憩云窗眠。
对岭人共语,
饮潭猿相连。
时升翠微上,
邈若罗浮巅。
两岑抱东壑,
一嶂横西天。
树杂日易隐,
崖倾月难圆。
芳草换野色,
飞萝摇春烟。
入远构石室,
选幽开上田。
独此林下意,
杳无区中缘。
永辞霜台客,
千载方来旋。

Sent to Wan Liu, the Royal Servant from the Peach Blossom Mound, the Paichao Hills, Anlu

I've lived with clouds for thirty years;
My free heart the great Word reveres.
Tho Fairyland's barred by East Sea,
I love phoenixes and cranes free.
Now back from the Peach Blossom Mound,
I'd sleep by the sill, sweet and sound.
I can talk with those on that ridge;
Monkeys to drink make a hand bridge.
In verdure they play for some time
And then the mountaintop they climb.
Two hills the eastern dale embrace;
A mound reaches for the west space.
Varied trees keep me from the sun;
The oblique crag does the moon stun.
The wild hue of the grass does change;
The wind blows vines to clouds derange.
I'd go in and a stone house build,
And attempt to reclaim a field.
In the deep wood I would abide,
Far, far away from the world wide.
Now to you, sir, I'll say adieu;
In a thousand years, I may see you.

* I love phoenixes and cranes free: The phoenix is a legendary auspicious bird in Chinese mythology while a crane is a symbol of integrity and longevity, only second to the

phoenix in cultural importance.
* East Sea: what is East China Sea today.
* the Peach Blossom Mound: in the Paichao Hills, 15 kilometers from Anlu County, in today's Hupei Province.
* Fairyland: referring to the fairy islands floating on East Sea, where Wordist hermits wish to go.

淮南卧病书怀寄蜀中赵征君蕤

吴会一浮云,
飘如远行客。
功业莫从就,
岁光屡奔迫。
良图俄弃捐,
衰疾乃绵剧。
古琴藏虚匣,
长剑挂空壁。
楚冠怀锺仪,
越吟比庄舄。
国门遥天外,
乡路远山隔。
朝忆相如台,
夜梦子云宅。
旅情初结缉,
秋气方寂历。
风入松下清,
露出草间白。
故人不可见,
幽梦谁与适。
寄书西飞鸿,
赠尔慰离析。

Sent to Jui Chao, a Recruit When I Am Ill in Huainan

O'er Wuhui I'm a cloud alone,
Like a vagrant far away blown.
No success I can accomplish;
All time and tide from me vanish.
My wills and plans all go away;
I'm growing weaker day by day.
The old lute is to the cask flung;
The long sword is on the wall hung.
Ee Chung croons his Ch'u song when jailed;
Hsi Chuang sings his Yüeh tune while ailed.
The country's gate's beyond the sky;
The way home's blocked by mountains high.
At dawn Ssuma's mound's gilt to gleam;
At night Tsu-yün's house haunts my dream.
My travel has come to an end;
Autumn hues to all bounds expend.
Wind blows to the pines, brisk and clear;
White dew o'er the grass does appear.
My old friends are all gone, no more;
In a dream who will with me soar?
May a wild goose send you my news
To relieve you of woes and rues.

---

* Huainan: referring to an area covering Yangchow.
* Wuhui: referring to an area of the southeast of present-day Chiangsu Province and the west of Chechiang Province.

* Ee Chung: an entertainer of Ch'u in the Spring and Autumn period. He kept his Ch'u hat and played Ch'u music even if being captured in Chin.
* Hsi Chuang: a minister of Ch'u in the Warring States Period. Though he earned a high position in Ch'u, he never forgot his homeland and groaned in mother tongue when he was ill.
* Ssuma's mound and Tsu-yün's house: the former residences of the two litterateurs, Hsiangju Ssuma and Man Yang, both located in the hometown of the poet, i.e., today's Ch'engtu.
* wild goose: an undomesticated goose that is caring and responsible, taken as a symbol of benevolence, righteousness, good manner, wisdom and faith in Chinese culture.

寄弄月溪吴山人

尝闻庞德公，
家住洞湖水。
终身栖鹿门，
不入襄阳市。
夫君弄明月，
灭景清淮里。
高踪邈难追，
可与古人比。
清扬杳莫睹，
白云空望美。
待我辞人间，
携手访松子。

To Wu, a Hermit at the Moonplay Stream

Of Master Worth P'ang I oft hear,
Who abides ashore, Cavehall near.
For life long, by Deer Gate lives he,
And ne'er comes to Sowshine to be.
Man and wife, they play the moon bright,
In seclusion, by the wild bight.
Their footprints are so hard to find;
They can compare with saints in mind.
Their tune I can hear but can't see,
Like the clouds floating beyond me.
When I go apart from this land,

Let's go to Red Pine hand in hand.

* Master Worth P'ang: a renowned scholar and hermit in the late Eastern Han dynasty, originated from Sowshine.
* Cavehall: a large lake in today's Hunan Province.
* Deer Gate: a mountain with cultural attractions to the southeast of Sowshine.
* Sowshine: Hsiangyang if transliterated, located in present-day Hupei Province, a birthplace of Ch'u and Han culture.
* Red Pine: a legendary immortal. As said, he could regulate winds and rains and burn himself without any harm.

秋山寄卫尉张卿及王征君

何以折相赠？
白花青桂枝。
月华若夜雪，
见此令人思。
虽然剡溪兴，
不异山阴时。
明发怀二子，
空吟招隐诗。

Sent from a Hill in Autumn to Guard Commander Chang and Wang, a Recruit

What blossom shall I pick for you?
A white blossoming laurel spray.
The moon is so bright like night snow,
Which, stirring, carries me away.
Tsuyu, inspired by the Shan Stream,
Set sail for Mt. Shade by the moon.
I'll go to you with dawning gleam
Lest in vain *Come, Hermits* I croon.

* laurel: an evergreen shrub with aromatic, lance-shaped leaves, yellowish flowers, and succulent, cherry-like fruit, a symbol of glory usually in the form of a crown or wreath of laurel to indicate honor or high merit, especially when one had passed Grand Test in ancient China. In Chinese mythology, there is a giant laurel tree on the moon, and it would never fall even though Kang Wu has kept cutting it.
* the moon: the celestial body that revolves around the earth from west to east as a

satellite, which appears at night and gives off shining silvery light, an image of purity and solitude in Chinese culture.
* Tsuyu: referring to Huichi Wang (A.D. 338 – A.D. 386), a renowned calligrapher with a carefree attitude in the Eastern Chin dynasty.
* the Shan Stream: a main stream with rich cultural attractions in present-day Shengchow, Chechiang Province.
* Mt. Shade: a range of mountains running from east to west, which is an important geographical dividing line in North China.
* *Come, Hermits*: a poem by Ssu Tso (cir. A.D. 250 – A.D. 305) in the Western Chin dynasty.

望终南山寄紫阁隐者

出门见南山，
引领意无限。
秀色难为名，
苍翠日在眼。
有时白云起，
天际自舒卷。
心中与之然，
托兴每不浅。
何当造幽人，
灭迹栖绝巘。

Sent to the Hermit in Purple Chamber in the Southern Hills

Outdoors, the Southern Hills I see,
Which carry me to reverie.
The charm's beyond wherefores and whys;
The verdure spreads before my eyes.
Sometimes white clouds float up to rise
And drift to the end of the skies.
My heart follows them as they go,
And my happiness does o'erflow.
When can I see the man profound?
I'd join him by the topmost mound.

* Purple Chamber: a peak of Southern Hills.

* the Southern Hills: a sight of great significance located in Sha'anhsi Province, regarded as a holy place. It is also known as the Southern Mountains, Mt. Great One, Mt. Earthlungs, the mountains south of Long Peace, a great stronghold of the capital, towering in the middle of Ch'in Ridge and rolling about 100 kilometers. It is the birthplace of Wordist culture, Buddhist culture, Filial Piety culture, Longevity culture, Bellheads culture and Plutus culture and is praised as the Capital of Fairies, the crown of Heavenly Abode and the Promised Land of the World.

夕霁杜陵登楼寄韦繇

浮阳灭霁景,
万物生秋容。
登楼送远目,
伏槛观群峰。
原野旷超缅,
关河纷杂重。
清晖映竹日,
翠色明云松。
蹈海寄遐想,
还山迷旧踪。
徒然迫晚暮,
未果谐心胸。
结桂空伫立,
折麻恨莫从。
思君达永夜,
长乐闻疏钟。

To Yao Wei, Climbing up a Tower on Birchleaf Pear Ridge After a Sunlit Rain

The scenes shine in the sunlit rain;
Autumn has to all come again.
I climb up the tower to look far;
How splendid the towering peaks are!
The plain rolls away without bound;
The hills and rills turn round by round.

The water hue by bamboos shines,
Bringing greenness to the old pines.
The sough from the sea blows my face;
Going back, I can't find my trace.
Time flies to the dusk, as if pressed;
I feel something muffling my chest.
Standing, a laurel band I make;
Why not follow you? Hemp I break.
Missing you, I lose a night whole;
From the palace comes a chill toll.

* Birchleaf Pear Ridge: 10 kilometers from Wannien County, in today's Hsi-an, Sha'anhsi Province.
* laurel: an evergreen shrub with aromatic, lance-shaped leaves, yellowish flowers, and succulent, cherry-like fruit, a symbol of glory usually in the form of a crown or wreath of laurel to indicate honor or high merit, especially when one had passed Grand Test, i.e. Civil Service Examinations for selecting government officials, in ancient China. In Chinese mythology, there is a giant laurel tree more than 1,500 meters tall on the moon, and it would never fall even though Kang Wu, a banished immortal, has kept cutting it.
* hemp: a tall annual Asian herb (Gannabis sativa) of the mulberry family, with small green flowers and a tough bark, the fibers from which are used for cloth and cordage.

秋夜宿龙门香山寺，奉寄王方城十七丈，奉国莹上人，从弟幼成、令问

朝发汝海东，
暮栖龙门中。
水寒夕波急，
木落秋山空。
望极九霄迥，
赏幽万壑通。
目皓沙上月，
心清松下风。
玉斗横网户，
银河耿花宫。
兴在趣方逸，
欢馀情未终。
凤驾忆王子，
虎溪怀远公。
桂枝坐萧瑟，
棣华不复同。
流恨寄伊水，
盈盈焉可穷。

To Senior Wang Seventeen, Magistrate of Squareton, and Ying Kuo, a Monk, Also to My Cousins, Youch'eng and Lingwen When I Am in Balm Hill Temple at Dragongate for an Autumn Night

At dawn I set sail from You Sea;
At dusk Dragongate does host me.
The waves rush o'er the surface chill;
Leaves fall into the empty hill.
How vast the sky extends, behold!
Hills and dales stretch, rolling and rolled.
The moon above makes our eyes bright;
The pines below our hearts delight.
The Big Dipper glows to the pane;
The Milky Way gleams to the fane.
So happy, a good night we spend;
Our merriment lasts to the end.
A phoenix reminds one of Lord;
I think of you near Tiger Ford.
For no reason, the laurels sough;
The cherry blossoms wither now.
Along the river flows my woe;
Into the valley my cares flow.

* Squareton: a county under Southshine, in the southwest of today's Honan Province.
* You Sea: name of a river that starts from Liang County in today's Honan Province and flows to the Huai River.
* Balm Hill Temple: a Buddhist temple located to the south of Loshine and next to

Dragongate Grottoes.

* Dragongate: one of the Four Grottoes in Loshine under today's Honan Province.
* the Big Dipper: the Dipper, a constellation composed of seven bright stars, which looks like a spoon in the sky.
* the Milky Way: a luminous band circling the heavens composed of stars and nebulae; the Galaxy.
* Phoenix: In Chinese myths, phoenixes, auspicious birds, unlike ordinary ones, only perch on parasol trees, and only eat bamboo shoots and pearly stone.
* Tiger Ford: name of a ferry on the Tiger Stream, near East Wood Temple. As is said, tigers could be heard in the hills when one sees off a guest by the stream.
* cherry: any of various trees (genus *Prunus*) of the rose family, related to the plum and the peach and bearing small, round or heart-shaped drupes enclosing a smooth pit; especially the sweet cherry, the sour cherry and the wild black cherry.

春日独坐寄郑明府

燕麦青青游子悲，
河堤弱柳郁金枝。
长条一拂春风去，
尽日飘扬无定时。
我在河南别离久，
那堪坐此对窗牖。
情人道来竟不来，
何人共醉新丰酒。

Sent to Magistrate Cheng on a Lonely Spring Day

The vagrant sighs sadly o'er the green oats;
The willow shade, so thin, in the stream floats.
The long twigs sweep the spring zephyr away,
Swaying, swaying, not restful for a day.
I'm south of the river, far from home there;
To face your window I can hardly bear.
You said you would come, but there is no sign;
Who will come to me and share Newrich wine?

* willow: any of a large genus of shrubs and trees related to the poplars, having generally smooth branches, and often long, slender, pliant, and sometimes pendent branchlets, a symbol of farewell or nostalgia in Chinese culture.
* Newrich: a county, built by Pang Liu in imitation of his hometown Rich County, in today's Lintung County, Sha'nhsi Province, famous for its wine, the best wine in the T'ang dynasty. Pang Liu, Emperor Highsire, born in Rich, rose from grassroots,

wiped out Hsiang's army and established Han, with Long Peace as its capital. As his father missed the beauty and wine of his hometown, Pang Liu made a copy of his hometown and moved the best brewers here, and ever since then Newrich wine has been well-known and has attracted generations of litterateurs to sing praise of it.

寄淮南友人

红颜悲旧国，
青岁歇芳洲。
不待金门诏，
空持宝剑游。
海云迷驿道，
江月隐乡楼。
复作淮南客，
因逢桂树留。

Sent to My Friend in Huainan

My siren confidante feels sad
For me in Balm Shoal, a stray lad.
No edict arrives from the court;
With my sword I loaf there to sport.
Sea clouds from the post go awry;
The river moon's neath the tower high.
I stroll here, Huainan's guest again,
For grand laurels I here remain.

* Huainan: an area in the drainage basin of the Huai River, first an eastern barbarian area governed by a vassal state of Chough called Choulai in Western Chough period, enfeoffed as Kingdom of Huainan in the Han dynasty.
* Balm Shoal: a shoal lush with fragrant grass.
* edict: a public ordinance emanating from a sovereign and having the force of law.
* the moon: the planet of the earth, which appears at night and gives off shining silvery light, an image of purity and solitude in Chinese culture.

* laurel: laurus nobilis, an evergreen shrub with aromatic, lance-shaped leaves, yellowish flowers, and succulent, cherry-like fruit, a symbol of glory usually in the form of a crown or wreath of laurel to indicate honor or high merit, especially when one had passed Grand Test in ancient China. In Chinese mythology, there is a giant laurel tree more than 1,500 meters tall on the moon, and it would never fall even though Kang Wu, a banished immortal, has kept cutting it.

沙丘城下寄杜甫

我来竟何事？
高卧沙丘城。
城边有古树，
日夕连秋声。
鲁酒不可醉，
齐歌空复情。
思君若汶水，
浩荡寄南征。

To Fu Tu from a Town Called Sandknoll

Why have I come, what am I for?
In Sandknoll I just sleep and snore.
By the town there are olden trees,
Which day and night sway a chill breeze.
Lu's wine can hardly make me drunk;
Ch'i's songs can't get me raised or sunk.
Missing is like the Wen profound,
Following you downstream, southbound.

* Fu Tu: Fu Tu (A.D. 712 – A.D. 770), a realistic poet in the T'ang dynasty, who has been regarded as "Saint of Poetry" in Chinese literature in contrast with "God of Poetry", Pai Li, the romantic unearthly being and Fu Tu's good friend. These two like two polarities complemented each other so well that they came often to be spoken of as one, "Li-Tu", who, more than any single poet, covered the whole range of human nature in Chinese literature.
* Sandknoll: a town in Lu, built by King Chow of Shang, in today's Giant Deer

(Chulu), Shantung Province.
* Ch'i's songs: Ch'i's songs were usually characterized by seducing flippancy, often to the accompaniment of music and dance with the same style.
* the Wen: the Wen River, 12 kilometers north of Mid-town in today's Honan Province.

闻丹丘子于城北营石门幽居，中有高凤遗迹，仆离群远怀，亦有栖遁之志，因叙旧以寄之

春华沧江月，
秋色碧海云。
离居盈寒暑，
对此长思君。
思君楚水南，
望君淮山北。
梦魂虽飞来，
会面不可得。
畴昔在嵩阳，
同衾卧羲皇。
绿萝笑簪绂，
丹壑贱岩廊。
晚途各分析，
乘兴任所适。
仆在雁门关，
君为峨眉客。
心悬万里外，
影滞两乡隔。
长剑复归来，
相逢洛阳陌。
陌上何喧喧，
都令心意烦。
迷津觉路失，
托势随风翻。
以兹谢朝列，

长啸归故园。
故园恣闲逸,
求古散缥帙。
久欲入名山,
婚娶殊未毕。
人生信多故,
世事岂惟一。
念此忧如焚,
怅然若有失。
闻君卧石门,
宿昔契弥敦。
方从桂树隐,
不羡桃花源。
高风起遐旷,
幽人迹复存。
松风清瑶瑟,
溪月湛芳樽。
安居偶佳赏,
丹心期此论。

A Recall Dedicated to Redknoll, Who Lived at Stonegate North of the Town, Where One Could See Hiphoenix's Trace. I, a Vagrant, Would Also Retire

Spring petals allure the stream moon;
Autumn hues spread to the sea blue.
Thru cold and heat I've been alone,
Lonely, lonely, I yearn for you.
I yearn for you south of the Ch'u

And from north of Mt. Huai I peer.
To my dream you've come, it seems true,
But we can't meet, for you're not here.
Before, we dwelt on Tower's east slope
And like souls divine shared a bed.
Twirling grass, at peers we sneered: Nope,
And spurned the court from the dale Red.
We went apart when we got old,
Going, coming, gleeful enow.
When I here in Swangate Pass strolled,
You were a guest there on Mt. Brow.
Ten thousand miles off, my heart hung,
My shadow the hills did detain.
With our long swords we came along;
Out of Loshine we met again.
The loud noise there did all dust raise,
Which made me so annoyed and bored.
Where was our way out, what a maze!
The haughty ones with a wind soared.
Then we went away from the court,
In nature we could farther look.
Farther looking, we had our sport,
And could peruse an ancient book.
For long would I to mounts retire
But my marriage has not begun.
Life is full of water and fire;
World affairs are many, not one.
This thought I could not dissipate;
A great loss I've seemed to deplore.
I hear you slept there by Stonegate;
How concordant we were before!

The laurels were where to abide;

No fairyland you would admire.

You had an outlook high and wide;

From hermits' footprints you'd go higher.

Across your lute blew a pine sough;

By the moonlit stream we had wine;

It was a good place, good enow;

Debaters could each to each shine.

* Redknoll: a Wordist and an important friend of Pai Li's. Pai Li met him at the age of twenty and once lived in seclusion with him on Mt. Tower.
* Tower: referring to Mt. Tower, located in the west of present-day Honan Province, one of the Five Mountains in Chinese culture.
* Swangate Pass: a pass of significance located in Shanhsi Province.
* Mt. Brow: one of the four Buddhist mountains, located in Ssuch'uan Province, named for its elegant brow-shaped silhouette viewed from a distance.
* Loshine: Loyang if transliterated, the second largest city in the T'ang dynasty, when it had about 800,000 inhabitants.

淮阴书怀寄王宋城

沙墩至梁苑,
二十五长亭。
大舶夹双槽,
中流鹅鹳鸣。
云天扫空碧,
川岳涵徐清。
飞凫从西来,
适与佳兴并。
眷言王乔舄,
婉恋故人情。
复此亲懿会,
而增交道荣。
沿洄且不定,
飘忽怅徂征。
暝投淮阴宿,
欣得漂母迎。
斗酒烹黄鸡,
一餐感素诚。
予为楚壮士,
不是鲁诸生。
有德必报之,
千金耻为轻。
缅书羁孤意,
远寄棹歌声。

Sent to Wang, Magistrate of Sungton from Huaishade

If from Dune at Liang you arrive,
Long kiosks you can see twenty five.
On both sides the barges have big sculls;
In the stream geese and storks make calls.
The clouds above sweep the blue sky;
The hills into the rills do pry.
Mallards fly from beyond the west;
At this I feel happily blessed.
Yellow cranes would Ch'iao Wang follow;
They could not leave their old fellow.
Now, dearest, I see you again;
Our friendship we can well maintain.
With backwashes the canal flows;
O'er this trip one endlessly rues.
In Huaishade I stay for the night;
Washing Mother greets me: All right.
She cooks chicken to go with wine;
So gratefully, with her I dine.
I am a gallant Ch'u fighter,
Not at all a trite Lu scholar.
I will repay her for her grace;
A crate of gold does me deface.
Oh, chap, I will send you my sore,
My sad song and this creaking oar.

---

* Huaishade: the birthplace of Hsin Han, a founding commander of Han.

* Liang: referring to Liang's Park, which was a royal garden of King Liang in the Western Han dynasty, abundant with rich cultural attractions.
* Ch'iao Wang: a magistrate in the Han dynasty, who was said to have magic power. As the records say, Ch'iao went to the capital to visit the lord half a month. The lord felt strange to see him so frequently that he ordered a grand scribe to observe Chiao privately. The grand scribe found that every time Chiao arrived, there would come a pair of mallards. When the mallards had been captured, they could only find a pair of shoes.
* Washing Mother: referring to the laundry lady who provided Hsin Han with food when the later commander was poor.
* a gallant Ch'u fighter: referring to Hsin Han, a founding commander of the Han regime. He had been poor and shown a good endurance of humiliation. Once a young man made fun of him and forced him to crawl through his legs, and Han did so without changing his expression. Not appreciated in pursuit of an official career or good at doing business, Han used to rely on an elder laundry woman who pitied him and gave him food without expectation of a return.

闻王昌龄左迁龙标遥有此寄

杨花落尽子规啼，
闻道龙标过五溪。
我寄愁心与明月，
随风直到夜郎西。

To Ch'angling Wang upon His Demotion

Catkins fallen, cuckoos begin their screams;
My friend to Lungpiao will go past Five Streams.
I'd consign my worries to the moon's care
So they'll reach Nightboy with a blowing air.

* Ch'angling Wang: Ch'angling Wang (A.D. 698 – A.D. 757), a poet in the T'ang dynasty. Most of his poems were about frontier life.
* catkin: a deciduous scaly spike of flowers, as in the willow, an image of helpless drifting or wandering in Chinese literature.
* cuckoo: the bird of homesickness in Chinese culture. It is said that during the Shang dynasty, Cuckoo (Yü Tu), a caring king of Shu, abdicated the throne due to a flood and lived in reclusion. After his death, he, the human Cuckoo, turned into a bird cuckoo, wailing day and night, shedding tears and blood.
* Lungpiao: an ancient county located in present-day Kuichow Province.
* Five Streams: an ancient name for present-day Huaihua in Hunan Province.
* the moon: the celestial body that revolves around the earth from west to east as a satellite, which appears at night and gives off shining silvery light, an image of purity and solitude in Chinese culture.
* Nightboy: once the biggest kingdom founded by southern barbarians in the southwest existing from the Warring States period to the Han dynasty. In 27 B.C., Nightboy was wiped out by Han and was made a county.

寄王屋山人孟大融

我昔东海上，
劳山餐紫霞。
亲见安期公，
食枣大如瓜。
中年谒汉主，
不惬还归家。
朱颜谢春辉，
白发见生涯。
所期就金液，
飞步登云车。
愿随夫子天坛上，
闲与仙人扫落花。

Sent to Tajung Meng, an Immortal on Mt. King's Hood

Then I lived by East Sea, the brine,
And on purple clouds I did dine.
I saw An, one thousand years old,
Eat a melon-size date, behold.
Middle-aged, he called on the throne;
Drear, he came back to be alone.
His complexion lost its spring hue,
And too early his gray hair grew.
Gold nectar he would like to try,
On a cloud cart, he would go high.

> With you on Heaven Altar I would be
> And let's sweep blossoms with fairies when free.

* Mt. King's Hood: one of the most famous mountains for Wordism.
* East Sea: what is East China Sea today, with an area of 770 thousand square kilometers.
* date: an oblong, sweet, fleshy fruit of the date palm, enclosing a single hard seed, a symbol of early fertility in Chinese culture.
* An: referring to Ch'i An, an immortal who sold medicine at the seaside of East Sea for a thousand years.
* gold nectar: in Chinese mythology, an extract made by alchemists, for one who would become an immortal, and in Greek mythology, the drink of the gods or fairies.
* Heaven Altar: unidentified.

忆旧游寄谯郡元参军

忆昔洛阳董糟丘,
为余天津桥南造酒楼。
黄金白璧买歌笑,
一醉累月轻王侯。
海内贤豪青云客,
就中与君心莫逆。
回山转海不作难,
倾情倒意无所惜。
我向淮南攀桂枝,
君留洛北愁梦思。
不忍别,
还相随。
相随迢迢访仙城,
三十六曲水回萦。
一溪初入千花明,
万壑度尽松风声。
银鞍金络到平地,
汉东太守来相迎。
紫阳之真人,
邀我吹玉笙。
餐霞楼上动仙乐,
嘈然宛似鸾凤鸣。
袖长管催欲轻举,
汉东太守醉起舞。
手持锦袍覆我身,
我醉横眠枕其股。
当筵意气凌九霄,

星离雨散不终朝，
分飞楚关山水遥。
余既还山寻故巢，
君亦归家渡渭桥。
君家严君勇貔虎，
作尹并州遏戎虏。
五月相呼渡太行，
摧轮不道羊肠苦。
行来北凉岁月深，
感君贵义轻黄金。
琼杯绮食青玉案，
使我醉饱无归心。
时时出向城西曲，
晋祠流水如碧玉。
浮舟弄水箫鼓鸣，
微波龙鳞莎草绿。
兴来携妓恣经过，
其若杨花似雪何！
红妆欲醉宜斜日，
百尺清潭写翠娥。
翠娥婵娟初月辉，
美人更唱舞罗衣。
清风吹歌入空去，
歌曲自绕行云飞。
此时行乐难再遇，
西游因献长杨赋。
北阙青云不可期，
东山白首还归去。
渭桥南头一遇君，
酂台之北又离群。
问余别恨今多少，

落花春暮争纷纷。
言亦不可尽,
情亦不可极。
呼儿长跪缄此辞,
寄君千里遥相忆。

Sent To Staff Yüan in Chiao County, a Recall of My Friend

With Draffknoll in Loshine I spent each hour;
South of Kingford Bridge he built for me a wine tower.
For much gold and jade we bought songs and cheers;
For months, once drunk, we despised lords and peers.
In the world I'd many a friend and guest;
Only you were my confidant, friend best.
This would not change tho mounts fell and seas dried;
We would not care tho our blood was splashed wide.
I went south there to pluck a laurel spray;
And north of Loshine, in mood you did stay.
Then we met again
And would close remain.
Close, we went a long way to Fairy Mound,
Where thirty-six streams flew and turned around.
Along the stream all blossoms burst and blush;
O'er all the vales a sough in pines does rush.
Riding steeds astride, we reached a plain great;
Warmly welcomed by Hantung's magistrate.
An Immortal called Purple Ray
Invited me to the flute play.
A fairy melody did Cloud Tower fill,

So dulcet, just like a phoenix's trill.
The band music did the long sleeves enhance;
So drunk, the magistrate did rise to dance.
He covered me with a gown, a brocade;
So drunk, upon his thigh my head I laid.
In high spirits, we would soar to the sky;
Having so drunk, each to each said good bye;
Kept off by hills and rills were you and I!
I came home to find my nest on the ridge;
You now returned, across Wei River Bridge.
Your fathers, like lions and tigers, brave ones
Held posts in Ping and fought against the Huns.
Fifth moon, we marched thru Mt. Great Go with pain;
Seeing wheels turning, we did not complain.
It had been long since we reached Northern Cold;
I was moved by your trust and faith like gold.
On the table were plates and dishes fine;
I did not want to go back, drunk with wine.
We wandered to a bend west of the town;
The river blue by Chin Temple flowed on.
Cheered by drums and flutes we rowed downstream;
The waving grass like dragon scales did gleam.
Inspired, we played with girls like blooms to blow;
Poplar catkins floated about like snow.
The belles were drunk against the afterglow;
The deep abyss did reflect their fair show.
The fair moon to these young ladies did shine;
They sang: a plumage dance should go with wine.
A brisk wind blew their song up to the sky;
And their melody around clouds did fly.
Where could we find such a blessed happy hour?

I went west to pay tribute: *Willow Bower*.

I could not reach the blue clouds over there;

I went back to the East Hills with gray hair.

By Wei River Bridge I met you again

And we two went apart from Cent Stand then.

If you ask me how aggrieved I might be,

Look at late spring blooms falling from the tree.

This I cannot fully explain;

That I cannot fairly attain.

I call my son to seal the verse for you;

A thousand miles away, you share my rue.

* Draffknoll: a winegrower.
* Loshine: Loyang if transliterated, the second largest city in the T'ang dynasty, when it had about 800,000 inhabitants.
* Kingford Bridge: a bridge of great importance in Loshine, which connected two prosperous blocks of the ancient city.
* laurel: an evergreen shrub with aromatic, lance-shaped leaves, yellowish flowers, and succulent, cherry-like fruit, a symbol of glory usually in the form of a crown or wreath of laurel to indicate honor or high merit, especially when one had passed Grand Test, i.e. Civil Service Examinations for selecting government officials, in ancient China. In Chinese mythology, there is a giant laurel tree on the moon, and it would never fall even though Kang Wu, a banished immortal, has kept cutting it.
* lion: a large, yellowish-brown or tawny carnivorous mammal (Panthera leo) of the cat family, native to Africa, Southwest Asia and South America, introduced to China, given as a gift to a Chinese emperor, in the Western Han dynasty.
* tiger: a large carnivorous feline mammal of Asia, with vertical black wavy stripes on a tawny body and black bars or rings on the limbs and tail, praised as king of all animals. The South China tiger (Panthera tigris Amoyensis), native to China, is probably the ancestor or prototype of all tigers.
* Ping: referring to an area covering present-day T'aiyüan, Shanhsi.
* Mt. Great Go: Mt. T'aihang if transliterated, meandering on the border of Shanhsi, Honan and Sha'anhsi.
* Chin Temple: the earliest royal garden located in Shanhsi Province.

* poplar catkin: catkin from dioecious trees and bushes of the willow family called poplars common in China.
* *Willow Bower*: a verse written by Man Yang (53 B.C.- A.D. 18), a great scholar, rhymed prose writer and official in the Han dynasty.
* the East Hills: in today's Chechiang Province, the hills where An Hsieh, a general and scholar, once live in reclusion, indicating a place for reclusion.
* Cent Stand: a vassal state enfeoffed to Ho Hsiao, the first premier of Han in today's Hupei Province.

月夜江行寄崔员外宗之

飘飘江风起，
萧飒海树秋。
登舻美清夜，
挂席移轻舟。
月随碧山转，
水合青天流。
杳如星河上，
但觉云林幽。
归路方浩浩，
徂川去悠悠。
徒悲蕙草歇，
复听菱歌愁。
岸曲迷后浦，
沙明瞰前洲。
怀君不可见，
望远增离忧。

Sent to Tsungchih Ts'ui, a Standby, When I'm on a Moonlit River Tour

A chill wind from the stream does rise,
And to the autumn trees heave sighs.
Aboard, you enjoy the pure night,
While setting sail on your boat light.
The moon turns around with hills high;
The water flows into the sky.

Above there rolls the Milky Way;
Dark clouds upon the forest weigh.
Backward, you see the currents rush;
Forward, you see the river flush.
To withered grass you sigh in vain;
Water Chestnut Song rings again.
The bent bank around the shore goes;
The moonlit sand to the shoal glows.
I miss you but I can't see you;
The distant view adds to my rue.

* the Milky Way: the Silver River in Chinese mythology, a luminous band circling the heavens composed of stars and nebulae; the Galaxy. As legend goes, the Milky Way maid, the granddaughter of Emperor of Heaven fell in love with a worldly cowherd and they gave birth to a son and a daughter. When their love was disclosed to Emperor of Heaven, he sent Queen Mother to take the fairy back to Heaven. While Cowherd was trying to catch up in a boat the cow had made with its horn broken, Queen Mother rived the air with her hair pin, so there appeared the Silver River, i.e., the Milky Way to keep them apart, and the fairy and the cowherd became two stars called Vega and Altair.
* *Water Chestnut Song*: a folk song usually sung while water chestnuts are gathered.

宿白鹭洲寄杨江宁

朝别朱雀门，
暮栖白鹭洲。
波光摇海月，
星影入城楼。
望美金陵宰，
如思琼树忧。
徒令魂入梦，
翻觉夜成秋。
绿水解人意，
为余西北流。
因声玉琴里，
荡漾寄君愁。

To Magistrate Yang When I Put Up for the Night on Egret Shoal

Dawn sees me leave Red Peacock Gate;
Dusk on Egret Shoal finds me wait.
The blue waves do the sea moon ply;
The bright stars accost the tower high.
Gold Hill sees its good magistrate
Like a nectar tree meditate.
Although in my dream you haunt me,
I feel each night like autumn be.
The blue water there knows my woe;
To northwest it does for me flow.

With the lute tune my love I blend
So it flows to you without end.

* Red Peacock Gate: the south gate of Gold Hill.
* Egret Shoal: 4 kilometers from Gold Hill, i.e. today's Nanking.
* Gold Hill: today's Nanking, one of the most well-known ancient cities in China, a strategic fort as a gateway to the sea, which has been the capital of Wu, Chin, and many other states or kingdoms, such as the six empires called Six Dynasties and has flourished immensely with increasing trade and travel.
* nectar tree: a fairy tree in Chinese mythology, which is twenty thousand meters tall and three hundred meters in circumference, often used as a metaphor for saintly people or beauties.

新林浦阻风寄友人

潮水定可信,
天风难与期。
清晨西北转,
薄暮东南吹。
以此难挂席,
佳期益相思。
海月破圆景,
菰蒋生绿池。
昨日北湖梅,
初开未满枝。
今朝白门柳,
夹道垂青丝。
岁物忽如此,
我来定几时。
纷纷江上雪,
草草客中悲。
明发新林浦,
空吟谢朓诗。

To My Friend from Newshore in the Wind

You can predict tides of the sea;
The rise of wind one can't foresee.
It turns northwest in the morning,
And blows southeast in the evening.
As we can't on a wind depend,

Our date sees my missing extend.
The moon is broken by the blue;
The pond teems with water bamboo.
Plums burst by North Lake yesterday,
Though just a few blooms on a spray.
The willows at White Gate today
Droop their wickers along the way.
Plants and grass know their date of prime;
To see you, I don't know the time.
Over the river snowflakes fly;
Faced with the grass, I sadly sigh.
At dawn from Newshore I'll depart
And I'll croon T'iao Hsieh's verse in heart.

* plum: a kind of plant or the edible purple drupaceous fruit of the plant which is any one of various trees of the genus *Prunus*, cultivated in temperate zones.
* willow: any of a large genus of shrubs and trees related to the poplars, having generally smooth branches, and often long, slender, pliant, and sometimes pendent branchlets, a symbol of farewell or nostalgia in Chinese culture. The best image of a weeping willow in Chinese literature is in *Vetch We Pick*, a verse in *The Book of Songs*, which is like this: When we left long ago, / The willows waved adieu. / Now back to our home town, / We meet snow falling down.
* Newshore: a shore located to the southwest of Gold Hill.
* White Gate: the west gate of Gold Hill.
* T'iao Hsieh: T'iao Hsieh (A.D. 464 – A.D. 499), an outstanding highborn landscape poet. He wrote a verse the poet mentioned when departing from Newshore.

寄韦南陵冰，余江上乘兴访之，遇寻颜尚书笑有此赠

南船正东风，
北船来自缓。
江上相逢借问君，
语笑未了风吹断。
闻君携伎访情人，
应为尚书不顾身。
堂上三千珠履客，
瓮中百斛金陵春。
恨我阻此乐，
淹留楚江滨。
月色醉远客，
山花开欲然。
春风狂杀人，
一日剧三年。
乘兴嫌太迟，
焚却子猷船。
梦见五柳枝，
已堪挂马鞭。
何日到彭泽，
狂歌陶令前？

To Ice Wei, Magistrate of Southridge, Whom I Meet and Greet While Rowing Upstream and with a Laugh Give This Poem

The east wind does to my boat blow;
Against the wind your boat goes slow.
On the river here each other we greet;
The wind does not break up the smiles we meet.
With prostitute and mistress on the spree,
You have no time or no regard for me.
You have three thousand hangers-on to shine
And three hundred urns of Gold Hill's best wine.
I hate I cannot share your glee;
On the Ch'u shore I stray to be.
The pure moonlight does me amaze;
The hill blossoms will burn, ablaze.
The mad spring wind will people kill;
One day, for three years I've been ill.
I'd go but my boat goes too slow;
The hermit's boat I yearn to row.
The five willows in my dream sway;
Hang your whip on a branch you may.
To P'engtse here when will you come
So we can like mad sing and hum?

* Gold Hill: present-day Nanking, one of the most well-known ancient capital cities in China.
* The hermit: referring to Huichih Wang (A.D. 338 – A.D. 386), a renowned calligrapher with a carefree attitude in the Eastern Chin dynasty. He once took a boat

to visit his friend on a whim on a winter evening.

* P'engtse: the county where Ch'ien T'ao (A.D. 352 – A.D. 427), a verse writer, poet, and litterateur in the Chin dynasty, and the founder of Chinese idyllism, who once served as the magistrate.
* the five willows: an allusion to Mr. Five Willows, alias of Ch'ien T'ao (A.D. 352 – A.D. 427), who planted five willows before his doorway when he lived in reclusion.

题情深树寄象公

肠断枝上猿，
泪添山下樽。
白云见我去，
亦为我飞翻。

To Mr. Hsiang, Dedication to a Loving Tree

The monkey's bowels break on the tree;
Their sad tears drop into my cup.
While the white clouds my leaving see,
They revolve for me, down and up.

* The monkey's bowels break: According to *On Science*, monkeys have a hot temper and short bowels. When they are sad, their bowels may break.

北山独酌寄韦六

巢父将许由，
未闻买山隐。
道存迹自高，
何惮去人近。
纷吾下兹岭，
地闲喧亦泯。
门横群岫开，
水凿众泉引。
屏高而在云，
窦深莫能准。
川光昼昏凝，
林气夕凄紧。
于焉摘朱果，
兼得养玄牝。
坐月观宝书，
拂霜弄瑶轸。
倾壶事幽酌，
顾影还独尽。
念君风尘游，
傲尔令自哂。

Sent to Wei Six While I Drink Alone at North Hill

I've never heard Freedom and Nest
Would buy a mountain there to rest.

If you have the Word, you are high;
Why worry somebody's nearby?
From the busy world is the knoll;
Here, you can hardly find a soul.
Out of your door you can see hills;
Many a spring gurgles from rills.
The high peak scrapes the clouded sky;
How deep the cave? In vain you try.
While mist on the stream decreases,
Haze o'er the forest increases.
Here we can gather blackberries
And we can raise calves and ponies.
Reading a book under the moon;
Plucking the lute to match the tune!
The pot tilts, spills out of the brim;
He drinks, his shadow behind him.
Why need you go to loaf around?
Why not drink much, in spirit drowned?

* Freedom and Nest: referring to Freedom (Yu Hsu) and Father Nest (Fu Ch'ao). They both were hermits of talent and declined to be king when Mound intended to abdicate the throne to them.
* the Word: referring to Tao if transliterated, the most significant and profoundest concept in Chinese philosophy. It is identifiable with the Word or Logos or God in the West, as there is an enormous amount of common ground in the great religions, concerning the most fundamental matters such as the One-to-many relation and the divine nature of the Creator, whatever it may be called.
* blackberry: the black, edible fruit of certain shrubs (genus *Rubus*) of the rose family.

寄当涂赵少府炎

晚登高楼望，
木落双江清。
寒山饶积翠，
秀色连州城。
目送楚云尽，
心悲胡雁声。
相思不可见，
回首故人情。

Sent to Yan Chao, a County Sheriff of Tangt'u

At dusk I climb up the high tower;
To the two blue rivers leaves shower.
Emerald spreads on every cold hill;
The town is tinted with green chill.
The Ch'u clouds float out of my sight;
I feel sad at wild geese in flight.
I miss you but I can't see you;
I turn back to see your eyes of rue.

* Ch'u: a vassal state of Chough, one of the powers in the Warring States period, conquered and annexed by Ch'in in 223 B.C.
* wild goose: an undomesticated goose that is caring and responsible, taken as a symbol of benevolence, righteousness, good manner, wisdom and faith in Chinese culture.

寄东鲁二稚子

吴地桑叶绿,
吴蚕已三眠。
我家寄东鲁,
谁种龟阴田?
春事已不及,
江行复茫然。
南风吹归心,
飞堕酒楼前。
楼东一株桃,
枝叶拂青烟。
此树我所种,
别来向三年。
桃今与楼齐,
我行尚未旋。
娇女字平阳,
折花倚桃边。
折花不见我,
泪下如流泉。
小儿名伯禽,
与姊亦齐肩。
双行桃树下,
抚背复谁怜?
念此失次第,
肝肠日忧煎。
裂素写远意,
因之汶阳川。

Sent to My Two Children in the East of Lu

The southern mulberries green grow;
The southern silkworms fall asleep.
My homeland's in the east of Lu;
Who can my farm till and reap?
Spring farming is too late to do;
Where can I go downstream? I'm lost.
A southern wind does my heart blow;
My yearning is to the tower tossed.
A peach tree stands east of the tower,
Whose twigs and foliage sweep clouds black.
'Twas planted when I left that hour;
'Its already three years, alack!
The tree's high, as the tower the same,
But I'm still in an alien land.
My daughter, Peaceful Shine by name,
Holding blooms, by the tree does stand.
Holding blooms, she does not see me;
Her tears drip down her cheeks, light, light.
My son, called Firstling Bird is he;
With his sister he's the same height.
They stand at the tree side by side;
Who can stroke their back with much care?
Thinking of this, I'm burned inside;
Nostalgia's more than I can bear.
On my sleeve I write down my roam,
As if I have now come back home.

* Lu: referring to present-day Shantung Province, the State of Lu in the Spring and Autumn period. Pai Li's children were left at the home of their mother's family in the east of Lu or East Lu while Pai Li was touring Wu or South China.
* mulberry: the edible, berry-like fruit of a tree (genus *Morus*) whose leaves are valued for silkworm culture, and the tree itself, first cultivated in the drainage area of the Yellow River in China about five thousand years ago.
* silkworm: the larva of a moth that produces a dense silken cocoon, especially the common silkworm from whose cocoon commercial silk is made. The silkworm was cultivated in 3,000 B.C. when Lace Mum, who was Lord Yellow's concubine began to raise silkworms and made silk.
* peach: any of the plant (*Prunus Percica*), bearing a fleshy, juicy, edible drupe, cultivated in many varieties in temperate zones considered sacred in China, often used as a metaphor for a young woman, as a section of a poem in *The Book of Songs* reads: The peach twigs sway, / Ablaze the flower; / Now she's married away, / Befitting her new bower.

独酌清溪江石上寄权昭夷

我携一樽酒,
独上江祖石。
自从天地开,
更长几千尺。
举杯向天笑,
天回日西照。
永愿坐此石,
长垂严陵钓。
寄谢山中人,
可与尔同调。

Sent to Chao-ee Ch'üan While I Drink on Mother Boulder in the Clear Stream

I carry a wine pot with me
And climb Mother Boulder alone.
Since Heaven and earth came to be,
Thousands of feet long it has grown.
I laugh skyward, holding my cup;
The sun glows west although still up.
I'd sit on th' stone for e'er I wish
So with Yan I'd angle for fish.
This verse I'll send you in the hill
So that we could together trill.

* Mother Boulder: a stone soaring from the Clear Stream, on which a track of immortal was said to be found.

* Yan: referring to Tsuling Yan (39 B.C.- A.D. 41), a renowned hermit in the Han dynasty. He showed his talent at an early age. After Hsiu Liu was crowned the emperor of Eastern Han, Yan was invited several times to serve the court. Though the emperor was an acquaintance of his, Yan declined the offer and chose to live in seclusion in the Richspring Hills.

禅房怀友人岑伦

婵娟罗浮月,
摇艳桂水云。
美人竟独往,
而我安得群。
一朝语笑隔,
万里欢情分。
沉吟彩霞没,
梦寐群芳歇。
归鸿渡三湘,
游子在百粤。
边尘染衣剑,
白日凋华发。
春风变楚关,
秋声落吴山。
草木结悲绪,
风沙凄苦颜。
揭来已永久,
颓思如循环。
飘飘限江裔,
想像空留滞。
离忧每醉心,
别泪徒盈袂。
坐愁青天末,
出望黄云蔽。
目极何悠悠,
梅花南岭头。
空长灭征鸟,

水阔无还舟。
宝剑终难托,
金囊非易求。
归来倘有问,
桂树山之幽。

To Lun Tsen, My Friend

On Mt. La Phu the fairest moon
Is with the clouds o'er the Kui blown.
If you go along the high way,
How can I with the masses stay?
If you give me a shine of smiles,
I'll have it for a thousand miles.
I'll chant to you when dusk clouds gleam;
Blooms fallen, you may haunt my dream.
When wild geese come here at this time,
You'd be strolling in the south clime.
Dust all over your sword and gown,
Your hair is scorched by the white sun.
The Ch'u path's greened by a spring breeze;
To the southern hills fly wild geese.
The plants and grass sway my sad sigh;
The blown sand veils the face awry.
I feel you've been away for long;
My rue's the pale of moon and sun.
Blown, blown, I drift along the shore;
My thought runs like a silent roar.
The nostalgia does weigh me down;
My tears drip off to soak my gown.

Gazing to the end of the sky,

I see yellow clouds downward fly.

How far can they be to my gloom?

South of the hills plums burst to bloom.

The sky broad, no birds in my view;

The sea vast, no boats on the blue.

My precious sword is laid to rust;

My golden bag I cannot trust.

If at last you could come to me,

I'd stand beneath that laurel tree.

* Mt. La Phu: an attractive mountain in Kuangtung where Surge Ko, a hermit in the Chin dynasty, used to live in seclusion.
* the Kui: a river that originates from today's Hunan Province and flows to Kuilin, implying Kuilin, a picturesque city in present-day Kuanghsi Province.
* wild goose: an undomesticated goose that is caring and responsible, taken as a symbol of benevolence, righteousness, good manner, wisdom, and faith in Chinese culture.
* plum: a kind of plant or the edible purple drupaceous fruit of the plant which is any one of various trees of the genus *Prunus*, cultivated in temperate zones.
* laurel: laurus nobilis, an evergreen shrub with aromatic, lance-shaped leaves, yellowish flowers, and succulent, cherry-like fruit, a symbol of glory usually in the form of a crown or wreath of laurel to indicate honor or high merit, especially when one had passed Grand Test in ancient China. In Chinese mythology, there is a colossal laurel tree more than 1,500 meters tall on the moon, and it would never fall even though Kang Wu, a banished immortal, has kept cutting it.

古近体诗二十六首
Old-new Rhythmic Poetry, 26 Poems

庐山谣寄卢侍御虚舟

我本楚狂人,
凤歌笑孔丘。
手持绿玉杖,
朝别黄鹤楼。
五岳寻仙不辞远,
一生好入名山游。
庐山秀出南斗傍,
屏风九叠云锦张,
影落明湖青黛光。
金阙前开二峰长,
银河倒挂三石梁。
香炉瀑布遥相望,
回崖沓嶂凌苍苍。
翠影红霞映朝日,
鸟飞不到吴天长。
登高壮观天地间,
大江茫茫去不还。
黄云万里动风色,
白波九道流雪山。
好为庐山谣,
兴因庐山发。
闲窥石镜清我心,
谢公行处苍苔没。
早服还丹无世情,
琴心三叠道初成。
遥见仙人彩云里,
手把芙蓉朝玉京。

先期汗漫九垓上，
愿接卢敖游太清。

A Mt. Lodge Ballad to Void Boat Lu, a Royal Servant

I'm the man from Ch'u, mad and bold,
Who once did that Confucius scorn.
An emerald stick in hand I hold,
And leave Yellow Crane in the morn.
To find saints I would go a long long way,
And in the famous mountains I would stay.
By Sagittarius Mt. Lodge towers up so high;
The nine screens like brocade spread to the sky.
The shade of hills with the light of lakes vie.
Before Gold Gate two peaks tower to gleam;
The Milky Way's hung over Tree Stone Beam.
The waterfalls afar at Censer gaze,
Crag to crag, peak on peak, all veiled in haze.
The clouds and the sun shimmer each to each;
The southern sky's too vast for birds to reach.
What a vast space between Heaven and earth!
The great river tumbles on to the firth.
Yellow clouds miles and miles chase the wind blow;
From the mountains the white waves carry snow.
For Mt. Lodge high I sing a song;
To Mt. Lodge high I go along.
At ease, I am so cleansed by the stone gloss,
Tho Hsieh's footprints are hidden by green moss.
I take elixir to keep off the world vain;

The great bliss and the Word I would attain.
Behold, the immortals mid the clouds stay;
Lotus flowers held in hand, to Lord I pray.
We've fixed a date to meet in the Ninth Sky;
Together with you, I would soar up high.

* the man from Ch'u: referring to Tung Lu, a hermit of Ch'u in the Spring and Autumn period, who sang with contempt in front of Confucius, and refused to seek an official career like him. It is said that Lu and his wife lived in seclusion in Mt. Brow and became immortals.
* Confucius: Knoll Con (551 B.C. - 479 B.C.), a renowned thinker, educator and statesman in the Spring and Autumn period, born in the State of Lu, who was the founder of Confucianism and who has exerted profound influence on Chinese culture.
* Yellow Crane: referring to Yellow Crane Tower, a famous tower in Wuhan, Hupei Province.
* Sagittarius: a Zodiacal constellation, pictured as Centaur shooting an arrow; the Archer.
* Mt. Lodge: a famous mountain, about 5,000 feet high, with historic, cultural and religious attractions, abundant with caves, ravines, grotesque rocks and cataracts, an especially sacred place to Wordists, located in present-day Chianghsi Province.
* the Milky Way: a luminous band circling the heavens composed of stars and nebulae; the Galaxy.
* Censer: Mt. Censer, a peak on Mt. Lodge, veiled with mysterious purple mist, hence the name.
* Hsieh: referring to Lingyün Hsieh (A.D. 385 - A.D. 433), a highborn poet, idyllist, Buddhist, and traveler, famous for landscape poetry. He once climbed Mt. Lodge and composed a poem about it.
* the Word: referring to Tao if transliterated, the most significant and profoundest concept in Chinese philosophy. According to Laocius's *The Word and the World*: "The Word is void, but its use is infinite. O deep! It seems to be the root of all things."
* the Ninth Sky: the empyrean, the highest of Heavens, the highest of the nine layers of the sky according to Chinese legend, and a similar notion in Dante's *Divina Commedia* in the west, *The Lüs' Spring and Autumn* in China and Buddhist Sutras from India.

下寻阳城泛彭蠡寄黄判官

浪动灌婴井，
寻阳江上风。
开帆入天镜，
直向彭湖东。
落景转疏雨，
晴云散远空。
名山发佳兴，
清赏亦何穷？
石镜挂遥月，
香炉灭彩虹。
相思俱对此，
举目与君同。

Sent to Huang the Judge When I Am at Lake Gourd, Bankshine

Waves surge in the Drown Baby Well;
'Gainst a Bankshine wind sails do swell.
The boat rows into the bright lake
And east to Shell its tour does make.
A drizzle starts from the west sun;
The clouds to the far sky do run.
The famous hills our mood arouse;
How can one his interest douse?
The moon hangs over the smooth stone;
The Censer is shining and shone.

> Merging with nature is our aim;
> Looking up, we will see the same.

* Bankshine: an ancient name of present-day Chiuchiang, Chianghsi Province.
* Drown Baby Well: a well built by Ying Kuan (? - 176 B.C.), a founding minister of Han, when he developed Bankshine.
* the moon: the celestial body that revolves around the earth from west to east, which appears at night and gives off shining silvery light. The wax and wane of the moon symbolizes the vicissitudes of life or of the world.
* the Censer: referring to a peak on Mt. Lodge, veiled with mysterious purple mist and looking like an incense burner, hence the name.

书情寄从弟邠州长史昭

自笑客行久，
我行定几时？
绿杨已可折，
攀取最长枝。
翩翩弄春色，
延伫寄相思。
谁言贵此物？
意愿重琼蕤。
昨梦见惠连，
朝吟谢公诗。
东风引碧草，
不觉生华池。
临玩忽云夕，
杜鹃夜鸣悲。
怀君芳岁歇，
庭树落红滋。

Sent to My Cousin, Glare, Staff of Fenchow

I have been out so long, alack;
When could I depart to go back?
The poplar twigs can be plucked now;
I climb up for the longest bough.
Spring hue tints all across the land;
Lost in nostalgia, there I stand.

Who cares about such things, alas?
I think they're better than gold grass.
I dreamt of Huilien Hsieh last night,
And this morn his poems recite.
The east wind does to green grass blow;
And there in the pool some weeds grow.
Lo, dusky clouds swarm in the sky;
Cuckoos to their night sadly cry.
While I miss you, spring will be gone;
Blooms falling, the court's a bleak one.

* poplar: any of a genus (*Populus*) of dioecious trees and bushes of the willow family, widely distributed in the northern hemisphere.
* Huilien Hsieh: Huilien Hsieh (A.D. 406 - A.D. 433), a litterateur in the Southern Dynasties period.
* cuckoo: any of a family of birds with a long, slender body, grayish-brown on top and white below, regarded as a bird of homesickness in Chinese culture. It is said that during the Shang dynasty, Cuckoo (Yü Tu), a caring king of Shu, abdicated the throne due to a flood and lived in reclusion. After his death, he, the human Cuckoo, turned into a bird cuckoo, wailing day and night, shedding tears and blood.

寄 王 汉 阳

南湖秋月白，
王宰夜相邀。
锦帐郎官醉，
罗衣舞女娇。
笛声喧沔鄂，
歌曲上云霄。
别后空愁我，
相思一水遥。

Sent to Wang, Magistrate of Hanshine

On South Lake the chill moon shines white;
To a night tour Wang I invite.
The chamberlain's drunk in the tent;
The dancing girls swirl up their scent.
The flute air rings over the shore;
The song soft to the sky does soar.
Our parting increases my woes;
My missing downstream non-stop flows.

* the chill moon: an image of loneliness and nostalgia in Chinese literature, usually in autumn. The moon accompanies Pai Li or Pai Li accompanies her all his life. He drinks to the moon, his cup, his shadow and the moon making a party of three; he raises his head to the moon and thinks of his hometown; he reaches for the moon while drunk and gets drowned before ascending the sky, astride a whale, as legend goes.
* Hanshine: a county in the T'ang dynasty, today's Hanshine (Hanyang), Hupei Province.

春日归山寄孟浩然

朱绂遗尘境,
青山谒梵筵。
金绳开觉路,
宝筏度迷川。
岭树攒飞栱,
岩花覆谷泉。
塔形标海月,
楼势出江烟。
香气三天下,
钟声万壑连。
荷秋珠已满,
松密盖初圆。
鸟聚疑闻法,
龙参若护禅。
愧非流水韵,
叨入伯牙弦。

Sent to Haojan Meng When I Return to the Hills on a Spring Day

My red ribbon thrown to the dust,
I call on Ashram at Green Hill.
Gold String shows me the Way August;
Blessed Raft carries me to Charm Rill.
The trees uphill form an arch flown;
The blooms downhill spread to the dale.

> The tope ashore tilts to the moon;
> Mist does the tower and river veil.
> The three realms full of airs of balm,
> A toll all the valleys combines.
> Prayer beads fill the whole of my palm;
> Dense and deep are the moonlit pines.
> The birds to sit for Dharma throng;
> Dragon King also comes around.
> Not a tuned stream that flows along,
> I can't echo Poya's lute sound.

* Haojan Meng: Haojan Meng (A.D. 689 - A.D. 740), a renowned pastoral poet in the T'ang dynasty, ranking next to Pai Li and Fu Tu in the entire galaxy of the poets of the glorious Tang Empire, but unfulfilled officially, he lived in reclusion almost all his life.
* Ashram: a religious rite of Buddhism.
* Gold String: In Buddhist sutras, Gold String is used to measure the borderlines.
* the Way August: a Buddhist term referring to the way of enlightenment.
* Blessed Raft: a Buddhist term implying Buddhist doctrines that ferry people across abyss of misery.
* Charm Rill: a Buddhist term implying a struggling life driven by endless desires.
* Dharma: truth and righteousness in Buddhist terms.
* Dragon King: Buddhists believe that Dragon King shields and sustains Buddhist doctrines, and according to Chinese mythology, Dragon King is the king of all races in water, commanding clouds and rains.
* Poya: a renowned litterateur in the Spring and Autumn period. He was good at playing the lute and his friend Tsuch'i Chung, a woodcutter, was good at appreciating his music. When Poya played his lute, Chung could always tell what he was playing about. After Chung's death, Poya broke his instrument, for there was no man in the world able to appreciate his music.

流夜郎永华寺寄寻阳群官

朝别凌烟楼，
贤豪满行舟。
暝投永华寺，
宾散予独醉。
愿结九江流，
添成万行泪。
写意寄庐岳，
何当来此地。
天命有所悬，
安得苦愁思。

Sent to the Officials in Bankshine from E'er Flora Fane in Nightboy

At dawn I leave the misty tower;
Saints and gallants o'erload the junk.
At dusk I reach E'er Flora Fane;
All the guests gone, alone I'm drunk.
I wish the Nine Rivers became
Ten thousand sad strings of my tear.
I write to my friends at Mt. Lodge
To tell you why I have come here.
Determined by what is divine,
One does not need to sigh or whine.

* Bankshine: an ancient name of present-day Chiuchiang, Chianghsi Province.

* E'er Flora Fane: a Buddhist temple.
* Nightboy: once the biggest kingdom founded by southern barbarians in the southwest existing from the Warring States period to the Han dynasty. When a Han envoy visited Nigthboy, the king asked: "Which is bigger, Nigthboy or Han?" This self-important question has been a laughing stock ever since. In 27 B.C., Nightboy was wiped out by Han and was made a county.
* the Nine Rivers: an alternative name for Bankshine.
* determined by what is divine: what is divine refers to Heavens or God or the Word, imagined as an omnipotent human, decides everything in the universe and beyond.

流夜郎至西塞驿寄裴隐

扬帆借天风，
水驿苦不缓。
平明及西塞，
已先投沙伴。
回峦引群峰，
横蹙楚山断。
砅冲万壑会，
震沓百川满。
龙怪潜溟波，
候时救炎旱。
我行望雷雨，
安得沾枯散。
鸟去天路长，
人愁春光短。
空将泽畔吟，
寄尔江南管。

Sent to Yin P'ei When I Arrive at the Border West on My Way to Nightboy

With the borrowed wind we set sail;
To next post we go like a snail.
At dawn I reach the border west;
An earlier exile's there, hard pressed.
The peaks along the banks rise high;
Mt. Ch'u breaks like an o'erdrawn tie.

All brooklets to the valleys rush;
All rivers are with runoffs flush.
The dragon hiding below waves
Comes in time and from drought all saves.
We have waited long for the rain,
So we can in good life remain.
Birds may complain the sky's too vast;
So sad, spring goes away so fast.
Along the bank I learn to croon;
See if I can fit your South Tune.

* Yin P'ei: an exiled official.
* Nightboy: once the biggest country of southern barbarians in the southwest of China. When a Han envoy visited Nigthboy, the king asked: "Which is bigger, Nigthboy or Han?" This self-important question has been a laughing stock ever since. In 27 B.C., Nightboy was wiped out by Han and was made a county.
* snail: any of numerous gastropod mollusks of terrestrial or aquatic habit having a spiral shell, a tactile foot, and a distinct head with eyes borne on stalks or tentacles, a symbol of endless pursuit in Chinese culture.
* an earlier exile: referring to Ee Chia (200 B.C.- 168 B.C.), a political commentator, litterateur, who gained his fame when he was young. When he served as an official, he was envied by those higher-ranking ministers. In 176 B.C., Chia was exiled to Long Sand.
* dragon: a fabulous serpent-like giant winged animal that can change its girth and length, a totem of the Chinese nation, a symbol of benevolence and sovereignty in Chinese culture.

自汉阳病酒归寄王明府

去岁左迁夜郎道，
琉璃砚水长枯槁。
今年敕放巫山阳，
蛟龙笔翰生辉光。
圣主还听子虚赋，
相如却与论文章。
愿扫鹦鹉洲，
与君醉百场。
啸起白云飞七泽，
歌吟渌水动三湘。
莫惜连船沽美酒，
千金一掷买春芳。

Sent to Magistrate Wang When I'm Back from Hanshine, Ill and Drunk

When I was exiled to Nightboy last year,
My glazed ink slab was laid there, for long dry.
And I'd an amnesty at Mt. Witch this year;
A glowing painting brush I can now ply.
The Lord must want to hear *Prose of the Void*;
I'd discuss the gist of arts I've enjoyed.
On Parrot Shoal I'd sweep the ground
And with you in deep wine I'm drowned.
The clouds are roused to fly to Seven Lakes;
The song on the water the Hsiang land quakes.

>   Why falter, do sell the boats to buy wine,
>
>   And spend all gold of yours on the spring shine.

* Nightboy: the biggest country in the southwest malarial area of China in the Han dynasty, a kingdom founded by southern people regarded as barbarians by Chinese. In 27 B.C., Nightboy was wiped out by Han and was instituted as a county.
* Mt. Witch: a mythical and religious mountain, which was thought to be a range of mountains in Sha'anhsi.
* brush: any of various writing brushes or called Chinese brush, widely used for writing or painting, invented or renovated by Tien Meng (259 B.C.- 210 B.C.), a general in the Ch'in dynasty.
* *Prose of the Void*: an article with a strong sense of Wordism written by Hsiangju Ssuma.
* Parrot Shoal: a shoal located in Wuhan, Hupei Province. It is named after *Ode to the Parrot* by Scale Mi (A.D. 173 - A.D. 198), an arrogant but upright man in the Three Kingdoms period. When Mi was banished to what is today's Wuhan, the magistrate gave him a parrot and required him to write a verse about it, hence *Ode to the Parrot*, comparing the parrot to himself.
* Seven Lakes: As said, there were seven lakes in ancient Ch'u.

望汉阳柳色寄王宰

汉阳江上柳，
望客引东枝。
树树花如雪，
纷纷乱若丝。
春风传我意，
草木别前知。
寄谢弦歌宰，
西来定未迟。

Sent to Magistrate Wang When I View Willows by the Hanshine River

Over the Hanshine catkins flow;
Facing east, a sallow I hold.
Willows by willows bloom like snow;
Like entangled silk they unfold.
My love for you plants and grass know;
The wind will pass you my note best.
Magistrate, it'll play thanks to you
And ask you when you will come west.

* willow: any of a large genus of shrubs and trees related to the poplars, having generally smooth branches, and often long, slender, pliant, and sometimes pendent branchlets, a symbol of farewell or nostalgiain Chinese culture.
* Hanshine: an ancient town, present-day Hanyang district in Wuhan.
* catkin: a deciduous scaly spike of flowers, as in the willow, an image of helpless drifting or wandering in Chinese literature.

江夏寄汉阳辅录事

谁道此水广，
狭如一匹练。
江夏黄鹤楼，
青山汉阳县。
大语犹可闻，
故人难可见。
君草陈琳檄，
我书鲁连箭。
报国有壮心，
龙颜不回眷。
西飞精卫鸟，
东海何由填。
鼓角徒悲鸣，
楼船习征战。
抽剑步霜月，
夜行空庭遍。
长呼结浮云，
埋没顾荣扇。
他日观军容，
投壶接高宴。

Sent to Fu, an Office Clerk, in Hanshine, Riversummer

Who says the river is so wide?
It is narrow like a white frill.

On Crane Tower you can see its tide,
Or on Hanshine County's green hill.
Your loud voice I can hear all right,
But your trace I can hardly see.
A call to arms you can well write;
Like Lien Lu, war wise I can be.
For our state we'd offer our best;
Our Lord gives no regards to me.
Grand Kingfisher's now flying west;
How could it fill up the east sea?
Drums and horns make a din downstream;
The warships have set sail to fight.
Drawing my sword, I tread moonbeam
And play it fast throughout the night.
With a shout I can make clouds stay;
My flair, like Jung Ku's, not yet shown.
Some day let's watch the troops array,
While having a feast with dice thrown.

* Riversummer: an ancient town tracing back to 350 B.C. when Sha-e was established and was officially renamed Riversummer in A.D. 589, one of the three towns that constitutes Wuhan, now called Chianghsia District under Wuhan.
* Crane Tower: Yellow Crane Tower, a famous tower in today's Wuhan, Hupei Province, built in the Three Kingdoms period.
* Hanshine: an ancient town and present-day Hanyang District in Wuhan.
* Lien Lu: referring to Chunglien Lu (305 B.C.- 245 B.C.), a sophist from Ch'i in the late Spring and Autumn period. Once, the State of Ch'i lost a lot of soldiers when they tried to retake Liaoton. Lien Lu wrote a letter and launched it into the city. Persuaded by the letter, the commander in Liaoton committed suicide and left the city to Ch'i.
* Grand Kingfisher: referring to Jayway. According to legend, a daughter of Magic Farmer was drowned in East Sea and turned into a bird named Jayway. It looks like a crow or jay, but with an annular head, a white beak, and red feet, carrying stone and wood in an attempt to fill up the sea.

* drawing my sword: alluding to Pai Li's swordsmanship. In his early youth, Pai Li exhibited a swashbuckling penchant, took to knight-errantry, and learned swordsmanship from Min P'ei, the universally acknowledged swordsman in the T'ang dynasty, and as Pai Li boasted, he even slashed several combatants with his cutlass.
* Jung Ku: Jung Ku (? – A.D. 312), a minister and renowned scholar in the late Western Chin dynasty.

早春寄王汉阳

闻道春还未相识，
走傍寒梅访消息。
昨夜东风入武昌，
陌头杨柳黄金色。
碧水浩浩云茫茫，
美人不来空断肠。
预拂青山一片石，
与君连日醉壶觞。

Sent to Wang, Magistrate of Hanshine in Early Spring

I hear spring's come without seeing her face;
I'll go and ask Wintersweet for her trace.
It reached Mightboom with the east wind last night;
The willows roadside sheen with golden light.
The water rolls to the end of the sky;
But you haven't come and I can but sigh.
On the green mount, a stone table I'll lay
So that we can drink there day after day.

* Hanshine: an ancient town, which is present-day Hanshine (Hanyang) District in Wuhan.
* wintersweet: Armeniaca mume Sieb in latin, a plant or shrub about 4 to 10 meters tall, bursting into bloom in winter to herald spring with small yellow or red flowers giving off thick fragrance. It is a symbol of elegance, solitude and pride in Chinese culture for its blossoming and fragrance in the coldest season while all other plants are still dry,

bare, and devoid of vitality. It belongs in "Four Gentlemen", the other three being the orchid, bamboo, and chrysanthemum, and one of the "Three Cold Weather Friends", the other two being the pine and bamboo.

* Mightboom: referring to Wuch'ang if transliterated, an ancient town and present-day Mightboom (Wuch'ang) District in Wuhan.
* willow: any of a large genus of shrubs and trees related to the poplars, widely distributed in China and most of the world, having glossy green leaves resembling a girl's eye-brow, and generally having smooth branches, and often long, slender, pliant, and sometimes pendent branchlets, which seem to be waving good-bye, or weeping amorously, or drooping for nostalgia.

江上寄巴东故人

汉水波浪远，
巫山云雨飞。
东风吹客梦，
西落此中时。
觉后思白帝，
佳人与我违。
瞿塘饶贾客，
音信莫令稀。

Sent to My Friend in East Pa from the River

The Han River far away flows;
On Mt. Witch thick clouds fleet, so pressed.
The east zephyr to my dream blows;
It lights here on its way to west.
I think of Whitegod now awake;
But from me you are far away.
In Big Pond there for business's sake,
Do send me your news while you may.

* East Pa: a county in the southwest of today's Hupei Province.
* the Han River: the longest branch of the Long River, having an important position in Chinese history.
* Mt. Witch: a mythical and religious mountain, which was thought to be a range of mountains in Sha'anhsi.
* Whitegod: an ancient city built by Shu Lordson (? - A.D. 36) in the Western Han

dynasty, located near present-day Double Gain (Ch'ungch'ing). It is famous in history as the place where Pei Liu, the Emperor of Shu, died in the Three Kingdoms period (220 A.D.- 280 A.D.).

* Big Pond: one of the three most important gorges of the Long River.

江上寄元六林宗

霜落江始寒，
枫叶绿未脱。
客行悲清秋，
永路苦不达。
沧波渺川汜，
白日隐天末。
停棹依林峦，
惊猿相叫聒。
夜分河汉转，
起视溟涨阔。
凉风何萧萧，
流水鸣活活。
浦沙净如洗，
海月明可掇。
兰交空怀思，
琼树讵解渴。
勖哉沧洲心，
岁晚庶不夺。
幽赏颇自得，
兴远与谁豁。

Sent to Lintzung Yüan Six from the River

On the river frost falls, now cold;
The maple leaves there still green stay.
The chill fall a vagrant can't hold;

The road before him rolls away.
In dense mist the waves wash the shore;
The white sun turns pale in the sky.
By the hill's grove I stop my oar,
So frightened with a monkey's cry.
The Milky Way turns on at night;
I get up to see the waves rush.
The chilly wind blows to my plight,
And I hear the river there flush.
The shore is so clean, with no stain;
I would play with the moon so bright.
I'm not waiting for you in vain,
Because your grace does me delight.
Cheer up, let's each other inspire;
To do something, it's ne'er too late.
For a quiet scene we may aspire;
Talking with you, I feel so great.

* maple: any of a large genus (*Acer*) of deciduous trees of the north temperate zone, with opposite leaves that turn red in autumn and a fruit of two joined samaras, a symbol of cordial love and good luck because of its bright fiery color.
* monkey: any of a group of primates usually having a flat, hairless face, elongate limbs, hands and feet adapted for grasping, and a highly developed nervous system, including marmosets, baboons, and macaques, but not the anthropoid apes, though monkeys and apes are used alternatively in Chinese, also used as a metaphor for somebody who is mischevious and shrewdly calculating.
* the Milky Way: the Silver River in Chinese mythology, a luminous band circling the heavens composed of stars and nebulae visible to the naked eye; the Galaxy.

寄从弟宣州长史昭

尔佐宣州郡，
守官清且闲。
常夸云月好，
邀我敬亭山。
五落洞庭叶，
三江游未还。
相思不可见，
叹息损朱颜。

Sent to Glare Li, My Cousin, Secretary General of Hsuan

You now help Hsuan's magistrate there,
Keeping so clean and free of care.
You oft tell me good is each scene
And invite me to Mt. Chingt'ing green.
Cavehall for five years sees leaves fall;
The rivers see me there tour or stall.
Missing without seeing lasts e'er;
Sad sighs may wrinkle faces fair.

* Hsuan: an ancient town, especially famous for its paper made of ebony wood, in present-day Hsuan, Anhui Province.
* Mt. Chingt'ing: an offset of Mt. Yellow, consisting of 60 peaks, rolling more than three miles and 317 meters above sea level, a mountain with many literary legacies, located in the suburbs of Hsuan, Anhui Province.

泾溪东亭寄郑少府谔

我游东亭不见君，
沙上行将白鹭群。
白鹭行时散飞去，
又如雪点青山云。
欲往泾溪不辞远，
龙门蹙波虎眼转。
杜鹃花开春已阑，
归向陵阳钓鱼晚。

Sent to O Cheng, Sheriff from East Pavilion at the Ching Stream

I stroll to East Pavilion; you're not there!
Over the beach flocks of white egrets fly.
The white egrets fly above in the air,
Like snow dotting the clouded mountains high.
Tho the Ching Stream is far, I would there go;
Waves turn like tiger's eyes at Dragon Gate.
Spring is o'er; azaleas are in full bloom;
I'll go to Ridgeshine to fish though it's late.

* egret: a heron characterized, in the breeding season, by long and loose plumes drooping over the tail, usually white plumage.
* the Ching Stream: a stream in today's Hsuan, Anhui Province, originating from south of the Chingte and flowing into the Ch'ing-I River in Ching County.
* Mt. Chingt'ing: an offset of Mt. Yellow, consisting of 60 peaks, rolling more than three miles and 317 meters above sea level, a mountain with many literary legacies

located nearby Hsuan, Anhui Province.
* Cavehall: a large lake in today's Hunan Province.
* Dragon Gate: Mt. Dragon Gate, located in Great Peace County, in present-day Hsuan, Anhui Province.
* Ridgeshine: where Sir Glare became immortal. Sir Glare, fond of fishing, once caught a white dragon. He felt scared and released it. Later, Glare got a white fish with a prescription in its body. He found all the ingredients and took them as elixir. Three years later, the white dragon came to pick him up onto a hill.

宣州九日闻崔四侍御与宇文太守游敬亭，余时登响山，不同此赏，醉后寄崔侍御

Two Poems Sent To Ts'ui, the Royal Servant, When I'm Drunk. I've Been in Hsuan for Nine Days, Where I Hear Ts'ui Climb Mt. Chingt'ing with Prefect Yüwen While I Climb Mt. Loud

其 一

九日茱萸熟，
插鬓伤早白。
登高望山海，
满目悲古昔。
远访投沙人，
因为逃名客。
故交竟谁在，
独有崔亭伯。
重阳不相知，
载酒任所适。
手持一枝菊，
调笑二千石。
日暮岸帻归，
传呼隘阡陌。
彤襟双白鹿，
宾从何辉赫。
夫子在其间，
遂成云霄隔。
良辰与美景，

两地方虚掷。
晚从南峰归，
萝月下水壁。
却登郡楼望，
松色寒转碧。
咫尺不可亲，
弃我如遗舄。

No. 1

Cornel does turn ripe the ninth day;
Doing hair, I find it grow gray.
Climbing high, I watch hill and shore;
The past and present I deplore.
I come to worship the one drowned;
I'm also one who loafs around.
Of all my friends now who are here?
Only you, my confidant dear.
Double Ninth's coming I don't know;
Let the wine boat follow the flow.
I hold a chrysanthemum spray
And with you, magistrate, I'll play.
At dusk I will go back and moor,
With cheers and shouts over the shore.
Two white deer draw a red dray,
Followed by those in full array.
You're among them behind the cart;
We are just like clouds kept apart.
I've missed the time and sites fine,
All charming dances and good wine.
Late, I return from South Peak tall;

The moon to the trailers does fall.
I climb up the tower to behold;
The pines turn green due to the cold.
We seem afar though we are close;
I'm like abandoned worn-out shoes.

* cornel: a kind of dogwood carried or worn on Double Ninth Day, as it can exorcize evil spirits, as is traditionally believed.
* Hsuan: an ancient town, a natural and cultural attraction, in present-day Hsuan, Anhui Province.
* Mt. Chingt'ing: a mountain with literary attractions, located nearby Hsuan.
* Double Ninth: referring to the Ninth of the Ninth moon, a day for the aged in Chinese tradition. There is a long tradition that people go climbing on this day, carrying chrysanthemums for their deceased dear ones and sprigs of cornel to exorcize evil spirits.
* chrysanthemum: any of a genus of perennials of the composite family, some cultivated varieties of which have large heads of showy flowers of various colors, a symbol of elegance and integrity in Chinese culture, one of the four most important floral images in Chinese literature, which are wintersweet, orchid, bamboo, and chrysanthemum.
* white deer: a Wordist symbol often seen in Chinese paintings; the animal ridden by an immortal.

其 二

九卿天上落，
五马道旁来。
列戟朱门晓，
褰帏碧嶂开。
登高望远海，
召客得英才。
紫绶欢情洽，
黄花逸兴催。
山从图上见，
溪即镜中回。
遥羡重阳作，
应过戏马台。

No. 2

The grandees come back from the sky;
Their five-horse carriages tumble by.
Halberds lined guard the scarlet door,
From the tent, one can see peaks soar.
You can see the sea, standing high;
From all around talents come by.
With ribbons they are in high glee;
Yellow blooms in hair join the spree.
The mounts in a picture appear;
The streams into a mirror leer.
Your Double Ninth verse I admire;
Have you passed Horse Play? I inquire.

* scarlet door: door of a palace or of a mansion, referring to a family of royals, nobles and powerful worthies.
* Double Ninth: referring to the Ninth of the Ninth moon, a day observed in memory of those who have passed away in Chinese tradition.
* Horse Play: a relic of a mound for horse play built by Yü Hsiang (232 B.C.–202 B.C.), Overlord of West Ch'u, after he toppled the House of Ch'in, located in present-day Hsuchow.

寄崔侍御

宛溪霜夜听猿愁，
去国长如不系舟。
独怜一雁飞南海，
却羡双溪解北流。
高人屡解陈蕃榻，
过客难登谢朓楼。
此处别离同落叶，
朝朝分散敬亭秋。

To Ts'ui, the Royal Servant

On the Wan Stream I hear monkeys' sad cry;
Away from the country, the lone boat I row.
I'm like a wild goose to South Sea, I sigh,
Admiring Twin Streams knowing they north flow.
You used to attend feasts in Ch'en's house grand;
A vagrant, in Hsieh's Tower I could hardly play.
Now I'm like a fallen leaf o'er the land;
At dawn from Mt. Ching't'ing I'll drift away.

* wild goose: an undomesticated goose that is caring and responsible, taken as a symbol of benevolence, righteousness, good manner, wisdom, and faith in Chinese culture.
* Ch'en: referring to Fan Ch'en (? – A.D. 168), a renowned minister in the Eastern Han dynasty.
* Hsieh: referring to T'iao Hsieh (A.D. 464 – A.D. 499), an outstanding highborn landscape poet. He once wrote a verse when departing from Newshore.

* Mt. Chingt'ing: a mountain with literary attractions, located nearby Hsuan, an offset of Mt. Yellow, consisting of 60 peaks, rolling more than three miles and 317 meters above sea level.

泾溪南蓝山下有落星潭，可以卜筑，余泊舟石上，寄何判官昌浩

蓝岑竦天壁，
突兀如鲸额。
奔蹙横澄潭，
势吞落星石。
沙带秋月明，
水摇寒山碧。
佳境宜缓棹，
清辉能留客。
恨君阻欢游，
使我自惊惕。
所期俱卜筑，
结茅炼金液。

Sent to Boom Ho, a Judge. There's Star Gulping Abyss Below Mt. Blue South of the Ching Stream, Where One Can Divine. I Moor My Boat at a Boulder

Mt. Blue towers, a sky wall like this,
And juts like a whale's forehead high.
It seems it bars the clear abyss
And gulps down the stars from the sky.
The sand holds the autumn moon glow;
The flow oscillates the green hill.
Such a good place, we should be slow;

The pure glow can keep tourists still.
Pity, you're not here for delight;
How disappointed I can be!
I hope to throw dice for a site,
Where you can brew nectar with me.

* Mt. Blue: 25 kilometers from Ching County, more than 3,000 meters high, in today's Anhui Province.
* the Ching Stream: a stream in Hsuan, in today's Hsuan, Anhui Province.
* whale: a cetaceous mammal of fish-like form, especially one of the larger pelagic species, as distinguished from dolphins and porpoises. Whales have the fore limbs developed as broad flattened paddles, hind limbs absent, and a thick layer of fat or blubber immediately beneath the skin. A whale is a symbol of great ambition, fortitude and uniqueness.
* nectar: also known as gold nectar. In Chinese mythology, it is an extract made by alchemists, for one who would become an immortal, and in Greek mythology, it is the drink of the gods or fairies.

早过漆林渡寄万巨

西经大蓝山,
南来漆林渡。
水色倒空青,
林烟横积素。
漏流昔吞翕,
沓浪竞奔注。
潭落天上星,
龙开水中雾。
峣岩注公栅,
突兀陈焦墓。
岭峭纷上干,
川明屡回顾。
因思万夫子,
解渴同琼树。
何日睹清光,
相欢咏佳句。

Sent to Chü Wan at Lacquer Ford Early in the Morning

In the west I pass Mt. Blue high;
In the south I reach Lacquer Ford
The water reflects the blue sky;
The woods see veil-like mist stored.
Water runs as if birds fast fly;
Torrents rush on like a loud pour.

The pool holds starlight from the sky;
The haze whirls with a dragon's roar.
Tso's railings on the stone loom,
And above there is Chiao Ch'en's tomb.
The ridge towers up like a high stack;
The river lures one to look back.
O Mister Wan, how I miss you,
Like, thirsty, I miss Nectar Tree.
When can we enjoy this bright view
And recite a verse with much glee?

* Mt. Blue: 25 kilometers from Ching County, more than 3,000 meters high, in today's Anhui Province.
* dragon: Though variously understood as a large reptile, a marine monster, a jackal and so on in Western culture, it has been esteemed as a fabulous serpent-like giant winged animal, a totem of the Chinese nation and a symbol of benevolence and sovereignty in Chinese culture.
* Chiao Ch'en: a man in the Three Kingdoms period. It's said that he revived six days after death.
* Nectar Tree: a fairy tree in Chinese mythology, often used as a metaphor for saintly people or beauties.

游敬亭寄崔侍御

我家敬亭下，
辄继谢公作。
相去数百年，
风期宛如昨。
登高素秋月，
下望青山郭。
俯视鸳鹭群，
饮啄自鸣跃。
夫子虽蹭蹬，
瑶台雪中鹤。
独立窥浮云，
其心在寥廓。
时来顾我笑，
一饭葵与藿。
世路如秋风，
相逢尽萧索。
腰间玉具剑，
意许无遗诺。
壮士不可轻，
相期在云阁。

Sent to Ts'ui, the Royal Servant, While I'm in Mt. Chingt'ing

Below Mt. Chingt'ing I abide;
I follow what I see as Hsieh's pride.

We are apart hundreds of years;
His grace before my eyes appears.
I climb up to reach the moon chill
And overlook my town and hill.
Mandarin ducks and egrets float,
Drink, peck and sing a merry note.
You're a crane on height in pure snow,
Sometimes you falter and slip though.
You look at hanging clouds on high,
Your heart soaring in the broad sky.
Your smile does often to me shine;
On sunflower seeds and beans we dine.
The world is like an autumn sough
That may blow plants and grass to bow.
Your precious sword worn on your waist,
All your promise you keep, so chaste.
A gallant should bear no despite;
Let's arrange to meet on Cloud Height.

* Mt. Chingt'ing: a mountain with literary attractions, located nearby Hsuan, an offset of Mt. Yellow, consisting of 60 peaks, rolling more than three miles and 317 meters above sea level, a mountain with many literary legacies.
* Hsieh: referring to T'iao Hsieh (A.D. 464 – A.D. 499), an outstanding highborn landscape poet in the Southern Dynasties period.
* mandarin ducks: duck-like love birds that appear in pairs, a metaphor for couples in Chinese culture.
* egret: a heron characterized, in the breeding season, by long and loose plumes drooping over the tail, usually white plumage.
* crane: one of a family of large, long-necked, long-legged, heronlike birds allied to the rails, a symbol of integrity and longevity in Chinese culture, only second to the phoenix in cultural importance.
* Cloud Height: a display tower for meritorious officials in the Eastern Han dynasty.

三山望金陵寄殷淑

三山怀谢朓，
水澹望长安。
芜没河阳县，
秋江正北看。
卢龙霜气冷，
鸦鹊月光寒。
耿耿忆琼树，
天涯寄一欢。

Sent to Shu Yin, Looking at Gold Hill from Mt. Three

I miss T'iao Hsieh atop Mt. Three,
Who here o'erlooked Capital Town.
In Rivershine you may find me,
Looking to the north with a frown.
On Lulung Fortress the frost's cold;
Over Magpie Fane the moon's chill.
My friend away so dear I hold;
Apart, we share a blessed free will.

* Shu Yin: a Wordist, Light-in's hanger-on, Sir Wood by Wordist name.
* Gold Hill: referring to Nanking, one of the most well-known ancient capitals in China.
* Mt. Three: a mountain located on the bank of the Long River.
* T'iao Hsieh (A.D. 464 – A.D. 499): an outstanding highborn landscape poet in the Southern Dynasties period.
* Lulung Fortress: a fort to the west of Gold Hill.
* Magpie Fane: a Wordist temple in Long Peace in the Han dynasty.

自金陵溯流过白璧山玩月达天门寄句容王主簿

沧江溯流归，
白璧见秋月。
秋月照白璧，
皓如山阴雪。
幽人停宵征，
贾客忘早发。
进帆天门山，
回首牛渚没。
川长信风来，
日出宿雾歇。
故人在咫尺，
新赏成胡越。
寄君青兰花，
惠好庶不绝。

Sent to Wang, Secretary of Chüjung, When I Go Upstream from Gold Hill, Pass Mt. White Disc and Arrive at Heaven Gate to View the Moon

The Blue River sees me upstream;
White Disc holds the autumn moon beam.
The moon beam sets White Disc aglow,
Bright, bright, like the mountainside snow.
At night hermits no longer start;

At dawn merchants will not depart.
To Mt. Heaven's Gate I set sail;
Looking back I find Ox Shoal fail.
The wind along the River blows;
The sun over the night mist glows.
Although you're not far, just close by,
I can't touch your hand, can't get nigh.
I would send you an orchid spray
So our friendship can for e'er stay.

* White Disc: a mountain in Tangt'u.
* Mt. Heaven's Gate: a mountain opposite to White Disc in present-day Anhui Province.
* Ox Shoal: an ancient town in present-day Anhui Province.
* orchid: any of a widely distributed family of terrestrial or epiphytic monocotyledonous plants having thickened bulbous roots and often very showy distinctive flowers, one of the four most important floral images in Chinese literature, which are wintersweet, orchid, bamboo and chrysanthemum.

寄上吴王三首
To King of Wu, Three Poems

其 一

淮王爱八公，
携手绿云中。
小子忝枝叶，
亦攀丹桂丛。
谬以词赋重，
而将枚马同。
何日背淮水？
东之观上风。

No. 1

King of Huai eight old men adored;
Hand in hand thru green clouds they soared.
Ashamed, I, of the pedigree,
Would like to climb a laurel tree.
Verse I never write by design;
I can Mei and Ssuma outshine!
When can I cross the Huai so grand
To face the east view, the great land.

* King of Wu: referring to Chih, a childe of the House of T'ang, the grandson of King K'o of Wu, who was the third son of Shimin Li, Grandsire of T'ang.
* King of Huai: referring to Peace Liu (179 B.C.- 122 B.C.), a childe of the House of Han, Wordist and litterateur. There were eight hangers-on of King of Huai, who became immortals in legends.

* laurel: laurus nobilis, an evergreen shrub with aromatic, lance-shaped leaves, yellowish flowers, and succulent, cherry-like fruit, a symbol of glory usually in the form of a crown or wreath of laurel to indicate honor or high merit, especially when one had passed Grand Test, i.e. Civil Service Examinations for selecting government officials, in ancient China. In Chinese mythology, there is a laurel tree on the moon, and it would never fall even though Kang Wu has kept cutting it.
* Mei: referring to Ch'eng Mei (? – 140 B.C.), a renowned verse writer in the Western Han dynasty.
* Ssuma: referring to Hsiangju Ssuma (179 B.C.– 118 B.C.), a representative verse writer in Chinese literary history.
* the Huai: referring to the River Huai, one of the seven rivers in China, between the Long River and the Yellow River, 1,000 kilometers long.

其 二

坐啸庐江静，
闲闻进玉觞。
去时无一物，
东壁挂胡床。

No. 2

The Lodge's calm as you sit and roar;
I hear to a higher place you'll soar.
Leaving, you leave nothing at all
But your stool hung on the east wall.

* the Lodge: an ancient river located in Anhui Province.
* stool: formerly called Hun stool, an armless and backless collapsible seat intended for one person, introduced to China in the Han dynasty.

其 三

英明庐江守，
声誉广平籍。
洒扫黄金台，
招邀青云客。
客曾与天通，
出入清禁中。
襄王怜宋玉，
愿入兰台宫。

No. 3

Lodge is proud of you, magistrate;
All in Great Peace say you are great.
You sprinkle and clean Golden Mound
To invite talents from all round.
I once climbed unto Heaven high,
So free in the court, far or nigh.
As King of Ch'u Hsiang was fond of Yü,
So I might serve you, King of Wu.

* Lodge: referring to Lodge County, that is, today's Hofei, the capital of Anhui Province.
* Great Peace: an ancient shire in present-day Hopei Province.
* Golden Mound: a mound built by King Glare of Yan in order to invite talents.
* King of Ch'u: referring to King Hsiang of Ch'u, who underwent the waning of Ch'u during his reign.
* King of Wu: referring to Chih Li, a childe of the House of T'ang, who inherited the title from his grandfather, King K'o of Wu, Emperor Grandsire of T'ang.